Antoine of Gommiers

Antoine of Gommiers
By Lyonel Trouillot

Translated by
Nathan H. Dize

SCHAFFNER PRESS
TUCSON, ARIZONA

*In memory of Jean-Édouard Morisset,
Michel-Rolph Trouillot, and Claude
Clément Pierre, seekers of the dawn.
To Esther, Anaïs, and Ariel.
To Jeanine Vaval, whose wisdom I
sometimes appreciate.*

Fè lanmou O Ayizan
O fè lanmou.
Make love, Oh Ayizan
Make love.

—A POPULAR HAITIAN SONG

Voltaire, like all lazy
people, hated the mysterious.

—BAUDELAIRE

"Humanity only confronts the
problems that it is capable of
solving"

—KARL MARX

Antoine of Gommiers, the oungan and seer.
They say he never raised his voice, he ate and drank little, only entertained sexual relations with his wife and mistresses on Thursdays in the even months, and on every other Wednesday in the odd months, and he ascribed to himself alone the name of his village on the map of the department, of the country, of America, if not the map of the world.

Thanks to him, Gommiers had no reason to envy the historical cities. Le Cap with its Citadel, Marchand-Dessalines with its forts, Camp-Perrin with its caves. Events come and go, some chase away others in peoples' memories. Monuments deteriorate, crumble, fall to the ground and often become piles of dust or meaningless stone pillars. History does not weather the passage of time the same as legends do.

Still, to this day, in order to instruct the ill-mannered in the virtues of discipline, to bring thugs back into moral order, and lunatics back to reality; in order to calm the reckless ardor of the frenzied risk-takers—the trapeze artists, speed demons, compulsive players, and greedy divers—looking to explore the depths of the ocean, highway robbers ransoming travelers, the sexually obsessed with their energetic and exaggerated spending, the stubborn politicians who cling to power, their eager heirs looking to deny their siblings their share of the inheritance; in order to sound the call of revolt in the heart of a victim foolishly subjected to the whims of a tyrant and to reinforce the lessons of common wisdom found in a variety of sayings like "the Lord helps those who help themselves," "those who live by the sword, die by the sword," and "you reap what you sow"; in short, to combat the many wanderings of people who end up on the wrong path in life, Antoine of Gommiers is the one on whom they call for assistance.

In anticipation of the gruesome consequences awaiting those guilty of excess, debauchery, and other character flaws, the threat was issued: "If you continue the error of your ways, even Antoine of Gommiers himself could not have predicted the misery that will befall you." Terror, oh Terror! What kind of unimaginable catastrophe could have possibly escaped the clairvoyance of the master? Doubt invigorates the threat. Since it is said that Antoine of Gommiers had predicted everything, the best and certainly the worst: love and love lost, famines, the World Wars, the assassination of a President before he was even born, the angel or the tyrant hiding beneath a baby's skin, great fortune, wimps, lulls, great thunderstorms, noble souls, miscarriages, false virtue, wrong turns, pretense, good, evil, and everything in-between.

The inhabitants of Gommiers could be proud of the scent of resin that carried through their clothing and hair, proof that man and nature are an extension of one another. The little trees having survived erosion, provided refuge for *their first loves, their friendship with the nor-easter, a fresh and lazy wind that flows up and down the seaside, accompanying those embarking, and welcoming those returning. But their greatest pride remains being the only people in 27,000 square kilometers to live in a place that gave birth to a man (but was he really a man in the ordinary sense of the word?) who became part of everyday people's language and speech.*

Of all the places in the country, Gommiers is the only one known throughout, finding itself implicated in every conversation, as much in the adventures and misadventures of intimate life as in the public sphere. In vestibules, alcoves, and worldly circles, in the times of the coups d'état and in the meetings of the boards of directors, found both in the Cité L'Éternel and Cité Carton where the mud sometimes piles up as high as a grown man and the trash heaps solidify along the coastline, drifting out into the sea and becoming small islands. Whenever there is a question of choosing one's path, of being self-assured or guilty of self-deception, there is always a voice around to say: "If you continue in the error of your ways..."

They called you "the master." I don't believe in the power of the divine, so I don't know what to call you.

I'm a child of tap taps, of alleyways, of the hustle and bustle of Grand Rue. A child of the dirty city. Here, to make youth last a lifetime, you need to be born either a whore or a gangster. They're the vocations that'll kill you the quickest, you'll rarely live to see your thirties. While others last a little while longer. The people. Not the vocations. Apart from gangs or hustling, as far as vocations go, if you lack an inventive spirit there really isn't a choice. After half a century of unemployment and uncertainty, of wait-and-see, of deprivations, those who are neither gangsters nor whores wind up dead anyway. You've got to have trust to give and a good dose of optimism, or resignation to find yourself a master you can faithfully serve. Here, we don't have the luxury of searching for reasons to justify our existence, and nobody has the resources to go on trusting any old person. Not even yourself. How can you know if you'll see tomorrow? What will you have to put up with? Here, how will you know when circumstances tell you: lower your arms, lift your feet, play dead or grit your teeth and get through it, book it out of here or don't move an inch. Take my best friend, Danilo. First, he was a police cadet, then a lieutenant for some gang leader, a lottery announcer, a used shoe salesman, an apprentice pastor at the Église de la Dernière Chance, a chacha musician and the backup soloist in a troubadour group, and so many other different things that by the age of twenty-five he could no longer remember all the lives he'd lived. His first name is his sole identity. Since he doesn't have a birth certificate and doesn't exist in the archival record, he often changes his last name. It's a matter of circumstance. Petit-Homme. Point-du-Jour. Israel. Durosier. Durosier, after the singer who spoke with a lisp when he talked. Because of the song he wrote about his parents hiding his shoes from him to keep him from leaving the house when he was fifteen and wanted to see the streets. Danilo's mother did the same thing, even though for him, leaving the house with or without shoes didn't make that much of a difference. Here, there are so many Danilos going by names that fit the truth of the moment. Here, you are what happens to you. And, seeing as it's never the same thing, life isn't just some loose ball of yarn that you can peacefully unravel. It's also not some small, lonely path you follow from one day to the next without curves and bumps. It breaks every day and you've got to spend your time tying the two ends together to make yourself into one whole person. Antoine of Gommiers, they say that you could predict everything. That you were never wrong. I know your legend by heart.

Franky did research. When he could still walk, he even went to Gommiers to collect testimonies. I know that he wants to turn them into a book. He's already found the title. Antoine of Gommiers. Plain and simple. As for the subtitle, one night when I was really drowsy, he told me it was complicated. We don't talk to each other often. So, with the sheet pulled over my head, I pretended to listen to him. He's looking for the mot juste to explain what he's doing in the book. "No one gives a shit about the *mot juste*, brother. I'm tired." But I didn't say a thing. With Franky, there are many words between us that go unsaid. When you talk too much, you say things that you shouldn't. In the alleyway, it's peaceful when it's quiet. As soon as people get to talking, because there's nothing better to do, misery twists the meaning of their words; a hello becomes an insult, and then quickly turns into a dispute. And when you spend your whole life hastily fending people off, your vocabulary tends to lack nuance and finesse. The people of the alleyways, they're not like Franky who only uses the *mot juste*. For his subtitle and for everything else. Memoir, hagiography... At "patrimony" I fell asleep. Patrimony. Memoir. Anchor. Lineage. Heritage. Pantheon. He traffics in words like these. The hardest part is when he combines them with adjectives the same way lottery players do with numbers. For patrimony, it's material and immaterial. For heritage, it's ethnic and cultural. In the neighborhood, all these words and concepts he knows are what make him different. As for me, I'm just Ti Tony and I only possess common, everyday words. But, without pretending like I can read the lines of the future, I've learned a few things. For instance, how not to conflate people with their legends. A legend is a bandage. You've just got to rip off the bandage and you'll see the wounds, open and buzzing with flies.

I liked Maître Cantave, the former director of the private school, Le Savoir. But not as much as Franky liked him. The classes weren't enough for Franky. He was the only one of us invited to the director's house, the cleanest one in the alleyway. Maître Cantave taught most of the classes, from history to mathematics, and it made him sad to have to turn away the children whose parents could no longer pay for school. He hated these final days of the month, which deprived him of half of his students. Money was not his priority. For a man who loved to talk, how frustrating must it have been to practice his art in front of nothing but a few empty benches. He sometimes loaned money to those who were eternally late on payments, just so that he wouldn't have to speak to an empty room. Then, he'd forget to ask for his money back, or pretend to. Wearing the same suit for twenty years. Eating fried potatoes and akra drawn from a bath of oil blackened by time and numerous encounters with an open flame. Who could bear to eat rotten food and wear a suit that wasn't much more than a bunch of patches? Maître Cantave sure could. But what would it mean to live without an audience? It's true, he spoke well. I especially liked his history class. The past flowed from his mouth and into the classroom like water that's crystal clear and safe to drink. He spoke with grand gestures. Historical figures jumped out of his sleeves along with stories and cavalcades, with declarations of principles we didn't understand, except Franky, who understands everything. All those people who held fast to their beliefs, threw their enemies into the sea, with their bravery and just causes, this transported us away from the present. In the past tense, everything is as beautiful as an element of style. This element of style business, that was another one of Franky's passions. Elements and styles. While returning our essays, Maître Cantave would repeat: "Man is the element of style." Then he would add, with disappointment in his voice: "There's only one man here. Well done, Franky. Well done, your use of hyperbole renders things according to their greatness." Hyperbole, damn, the amount of time it took for me to understand what that word meant.

From the time he was little, Franky understood everything right away. At school, all it did was give the jealous kids a pretext for beating his ass to verify that there was indeed a man behind those elements of style and honors ribbons. But I had the overrated reputation of a fighter. I was friends with Danilo who was a real fighter and Pépé the Moron, who struck fear in the hearts of everyone. Danilo and I fought like kids fighting other kids. We were often victorious, but in the end, there were no broken bones or anything. We were the champions of our childhood weight division. Completely innocent fighters. Our adversaries only took blows to their sense of pride. All you had to do was knock them down or wait until they surrendered, out of shame or boredom. Pépé never fought with the innocence of childhood. His blows were meant to destroy. And weapons were his specialty: a frenn—a makeshift knife, a razorblade, or a pair of brass knuckles. Everyone called him Pépé the Moron. He only knew how to write in the color red. His essays were the scars he wrote on other kids' bodies.

Franky never fought. Franky did his homework at night in our half of the bedroom. He spent a lot of time on it, re-reading his assignments a hundred times over. I sometimes saw him stop writing, pausing pensively, his pencil in hand, and I would ask him:

"What's up?"

"I'm looking for the *mot juste.*"

Then he would start writing again, smiling. I imagine he found it, his mot juste. In our essays that we wrote at the last-minute right before walking into the classroom, the rest of us used everyday language, words commonly used in the alleyway: "kolonn" for friend, "familia" for gang, "estéra" for scandal, and Maître Cantave reproached us for talking like everyone else. The insult was lost on us. It only made us feel prouder. By living through his books, Maître Cantave had forgotten that in the alleyway, nobody ever wrote a thing; it was the only world we knew. But it's true, rhetoric was Franky's business, along with all the other things and places he liked to talk about. I never understood how so many words and worlds could enter our bedroom. Maître Cantave greeted his presence like a gift from the heavens, the one and only proof that his teaching meant something. Franky and Maître Cantave; or, how one single child could be a Salvation Army for a lonely adult. They traveled together in the past, so they were essentially the same age. It's almost like Franky had two brothers, Maître Cantave and me. Each one had their own passion. Theirs was to travel back in time. Maître Cantave refused to play card games with the old folks. And Franky never joined in ours. Maître Cantave and

Franky were a crew. Full steam ahead, sailor! Next stop, the past. The place where everything becomes beautiful—even the dead. In the past, the dead are beautiful, and they wave, "hey, have you noticed me?" from up on high, with their rhetorical devices. They're always standing or on horseback, with their big hats, medals, and epaulettes. They didn't all have the luxury of a state funeral or even one in a cathedral, the right to an ode or an epitaph, but at the same time it's a nice homage to have your name in a textbook. The past is where the dead come to life and turn into heroes. Luckily for them that historians only include the strategists, the geniuses, and the army generals. If they opened "the pantheon" to them, the little soldiers would line up and push each other at the entrance like they do at city hall when they organize a free distribution of rice and flour. Here, we're not much more than little soldiers killing each other in search of rice and flour. Our dead aren't heroes, they're just cadavers. By the time we gather their bodies, another life force unceremoniously swarms what remains of their flesh. A cadaver is not a human. It's a composite material with a short lifespan, a hybrid form with a stench. There's nothing honorable about its fate: the fire, insects, or the trash. Sometimes all three at the same time. The dead who emerge from the past, did they live their lives in stages, were they cadavers before becoming heroes? Maître Cantave taught us that we had to progress our way from one stage to the next. His motto was, "corners are something we should never cut." And the promise of an apotheosis when patience runs dry. Then, one day, he also became a cadaver. He had this bad habit of wandering at night to escape the stench of the alleyways. The little soldiers of the alleyways don't breathe in high quality air. There's no use opening the windows. Outside also lacks space. If you leave the window open, you take in a huge whiff of that concentrated, rotten smell right in the face.

Maître Cantave, he was walking at night searching for a bit of open space to breathe. When wanderings and violence quarrel with one another for a share of the night, violence always wins. Pépé the Moron descended upon him. Then he cut off his arms with a meat cleaver, ridding him of the contents of his sleeves, in remembrance of the time when Maître Cantave treated him like a moron in his middle school class. You couldn't really say it was nothing but roses between Pépé and the private school, Le Savoir. He didn't have the money to pay for it and was sent home at the end of every month. And when he was there, since he didn't understand a thing, Maître Cantave would say: "Young man, you're full of nothing but gaps." We all have our gaps. The way Maître Cantave would put it, we could have built a mountain out of the things that we refused to learn. But Pépé, he took the cake, incapable of repeating the answers that we whispered into his ear, nor to properly copy the dates and formulas we passed him on slips of paper. One day, just like Abraham, he said to himself, "Enough." He went from being the last in the class to a gang leader, from a knife to an axe and from a razor to a revolver. He filled in his gaps, cutting corners and Maître Cantave's body, too, which did not turn into a hero. Goodbye, Professor.

Antoine of Gommiers, they say that you're never wrong

and that you've seen everything to come. As for Ti Tony of Grand Rue, your great-great-great nephew, Maître Cantave and Pépé the Moron, and the bodies with severed arms, did you see all of that coming, too?

In Antoine of Gommier's time, before the Second World War, dozens of beggars in search of miracles and prophecies, natives of the country's five departments, along with a few foreigners, embattled politicians, and renowned artists secretly disembarking from a ship en route from North America wanted to hear their destiny straight from the mouth of the man from Gommiers. Half of these visiters arrived by land. It took more than twenty-four hours to travel from the capital to Gommiers. The master mostly received people in the morning, since Gommiers offered nowhere to sleep. Folks had to travel to Jérémie, spend the night, and retrace their steps early the next morning. Transportation for the less fortunate travelers was ensured all the way to Jérémie by aging buses belonging to two companies: La Belle Griffonne and the Jérémiades. The editor-in-chief of the newspaper "Ad Libitum", a broadside periodical based out of Jérémie, suffered from obesity and chronic back pain—so he never passed up an opportunity to condemn the travel conditions. He published his journal at will, three times a year or ten days in a row, in accordance with the amount of gossip he collected in the capital regarding the mundane details of life, as well as the ascendancy or the decline of political personalities. Road conditions were a recurring subject. As a lover of biblical and classical references, he had written in the March 1936 issue of the paper that he, "being neither Jesus, nor Orpheus" had experienced in one voyage "the descent into the Inferno and the climbing of mount Golgotha." The newspaper did not release an issue in April, returning only in May for the occasion of Mother's Day. In his editorial, the chronicler vowed to put an end to his long silence in the name of the women of Jérémie cursed with having to walk along "this slave route" to visit their children off studying at universities in Port-au-Prince. In reality, he thought it was smart to keep a low profile for some time after leveling too direct an attack on the Minister of Public Works. And the secret motivation for pleading the cause of "those poor mothers" was part of his assiduous courtship of a widow whose two daughters were boarders at a finishing school in the capital.

I've never been to Gommiers. I wasn't interested in going, even when Franky returned, smiling, with his backpack weighted down by mangoes, sapodillas, and large manila envelopes packed with legends and information. He went looking for the past, and he found it. Antoinette really was the great Antoine's great-great niece. And what now? I said to him, kolonn, why are you chasing after these vain, far-out subjects? We've only got a short amount of time, and you want to spend it recounting a tale of loss? But Franky steadfastly believed that when we encounter folks like us, tossed into some corner of Grand Rue, we need antecedents. "Whether wandering or staying put, nobody can live without landmarks." As if by going back in time, it would open the gates of heaven! Antoinette's the one who put these crazy ideas into his head. Antoinette didn't have many ideas, but the few that she possessed were impossible to dislodge. She believed that one day she would win the local lottery, the bòlèt! All three prizes: fifty, fifteen, and ten. She believed that happy surprises exist, but you shouldn't expect them because then they're no longer surprises. She believed that life in Gommiers was better than life here. She repeated that every day. "It's so much better in Gommiers." First of all, this wasn't much of a revelation. I imagine that most places in the world are better than here. Otherwise, we'd be billions of miserable human brothers and sisters rotting in alleyways leading to a dusty, bipolar street, crowded by day, and deserted by night. We call it Grand Rue, but its real name is Boulevard Jean-Jacques Dessalines. I can tell you what Boulevard Jean-Jacques Dessalines is. By day, it's the coming and going of tap taps and all manner of dealings, some more illegal than others. Every day, another business shutters its doors. On Boulevard Jean-Jacques Dessalines, even illegality no longer feeds her man. By night, there are a few businesses left, these even more illegal than those by day. Just a few clients and a few whores, old and wrinkled enough to be their clients' mothers. By night, what's left on Boulevard Jean-Jacques Dessalines is a long straight line inhabited by fear, a few screams, and the sound of bullets. So, there's no reason to be surprised that it's better somewhere else.

That's no reason for Antoinette to sell us the village of Gommiers like it's some miraculous garden, the happiest place on God's green earth, where only good fortune grows. Where have we ever heard that happiness packs his bags to go and settle somewhere else? Happiness doesn't like to travel, except in the resort industry, so that he can take pictures of himself and fashion memories. Otherwise, happiness stays put. And when happiness visits other people, he travels light, wearing a tee-shirt, Bermuda shorts, and a camera along with the things inspiring his curiosity, then only to return home to celebrate his differences. Sometimes happiness comes around here. In shorts. Stepping down from an an all-terrain vehicle packed down with equipment. Long enough for an investigation or a reportage, or to buy works of art. He's so gullible, happiness. And since happiness isn't used to witnessing misery in all its colors, he mistakes misery for art, especially when misery plays with trash as a means of recycling. Danilo gets around more than we do. Danilo says there are bars that foreigners visit, places where locals with dreadlocks hang out looking for a chance to score a visa so they can go somewhere else to pose as works of art.

Franky's also quite gullible. He loved Antoinette the way you drink water from a source. To return to the source, that was another one of her delusions. The water in a source is pure. As a source, Antoinette could neither be proven wrong, nor was she capable of telling us a lie. If Antoinette was a source, she had long since run dry. You could see from her skin that her body lacked water. Apart from the tears shed as she awakened on sad mornings. When her dreams at night were bad and she dared to cry, believing that we were still asleep. Antoinette was so afraid of letting herself go that she didn't dare shed a tear. One day I asked her, if Gommiers is so much better, why did this Grandma Hortense, whom we'd never met, come to the capital without any luggage or a penny to her name to become a prostitute. She slapped me. I shouldn't have said "to become a prostitute." I don't know if this Grandma Hortense truly existed, so I'm unaware of all the pursuits she might've explored. Antoinette claims she was a beautiful person. That a quarrel between some of Antoine's nephews drove her to Port-au-Prince. A proud, modest, and beautiful person. A rightful heir to the Master. A rightful daughter of Gommiers, the land blessed by the gods. I smiled, skeptically. When adults ramble, they react poorly to smiling children. And then come the beatings. For Antoinette, it was either Gommiers or a beating. Gommiers and beatings. She had never been to Gommiers before. Images of places that matter manage to reach us in the alleyways. There are always pictures and movies for those who own a TV. Antoinette didn't even own a picture of Gommiers. All she knew were Grandma Hortense's stories. I called them tales. I say Grandma Hortense, but I only know of her existence from Antoinette's mouth. When we were born, there was only really Antoinette. We had no kin, no grandparents. All we know about our relatives are the names that came from Antoinette's mouth. Franky thinks that words can make something real. If his belief were in the future, I'd say that's still possible. Who knows, perhaps future inventions can lie hidden behind words. Like Antoinette would say, a happy surprise. Even with happy surprises, we have the right to despair if they take too long to arrive. For the folks in the alleyways, tomorrow hasn't ceased to look like yesterday in a long while. Who knows, everything happens someday, right? For Franky, it's not like that at all, he wants to invent the past. When he was little, he'd already developed the bad habit of writing everything down in a notebook. Along with another vice, this way of seeing people differently than they were. Larger than life. In blues. With glimmering halos. He often referred to Maître Cantave, who said: "You mustn't see the individual, but rather their light or their aura." I have no idea what an aura is and the only lights I can see are the sun as it burns the top of my head and the yellow glow of the lightbulb at night when Franky's working on Antoine's life story. I loved Antoinette, too. In another way, without an aura or an element of style. In a life that isn't really a life, which she lived along with us, for us in the shadows. In real, everyday life. No need for a Grandma Hortense. Or for some Antoine who sees everything. "Yes, I loved you. No need to add fables or to apply some salve. I could've escaped the beatings. Or I could've grabbed your arm, it wasn't so strong. The beatings, I let you administer them. It was the proof of my affection. I loved you for the poor little woman you were. You experienced unbridled misery. A permanent state of aging. A routine constantly turning inward. A slow death whose truth consisted of losing the bòlèt and searching for the balance between one's burden and one's deprivations. I loved you even with the beatings. Everything serves a purpose. The beatings, they were your form of revolt. For want of an aura and light, they were your little bit of rage. Luckily, I wasn't docile like Franky, otherwise you would've died without ever having the chance to claim your right to anger. Let it all out, Manman. Two children and your little traveling store. Three mouths to feed, even though I never actually saw you eat a thing. You were content with tasting our food like it cost you money to bring the spoon to your lips. When it was time to eat, to leave most of the food for us to eat, you acted like your mind was somewhere else. Franky thought you were an angel. And angels, they don't eat. But me, I knew."

Now that Antoinette is dead, I have the nerve to explain things to her. But the insects have eaten away at the dead, destroying their ability to hear. And all that you can tell them, all that we can tell them, all that you can offer them are deferred hopes, echo-less confessions. When we were still children, there was nothing beautiful about Antoinette's appearance. Maybe her legs. Only a memory of her elegance or liveliness. For men in the alleyways, legs are enough. They followed her around like flies. Offered to move in with her. To take care of us. Sure. Like Danilo's stepfather took care of him by branding his back with an iron. Her legs, they were the only asset Antoinette possessed to attract the flies. Prayers and threats. Promises, promises... When flies pick up the scent of a wound, a breeding ground where they can spit out their larvae, they never quit buzzing. These fly-men buzzed all around her. She resisted their advances. Antoine's great-great niece couldn't just shack up with some nobody and, in the alleyway, the only men around were nobodies. Men of humble origins and unemployed. Or hard-working brutes who drink a sad alcohol at night and whose heavy hands had already destroyed all their furniture. So, all that's left for them to beat on is their wife and children. For me and Franky, the only fatherly presence in our lives was the absence of a stepfather. And then, one day it all stopped. The advances, and the buzzing. Antoinette's legs withered too quickly, and the men left her alone. In the alleyway, generall speaking, if men, including the most broke and least attractive among them, stop chasing after a woman, it means that she's about to disappear. I loved Antoinette for who she was. A grievous woman standing on two tired legs who couldn't even attract a fly. And would soon die. After every beating, she was beset with grief, trying to pull me in closer to her. I pushed her away. She thought I hated her, and it only made her even more sad. "I didn't hate you. It's just this tenderness layered with guilt, it always rang false. Like an excuse. Let it all out, Manman." With all the worries she had, there was no need for her to waste her time with affection. "It's okay Manman, if all I can do for you is allow you to beat on me... There's no need for tears or apologies between us. You've already killed yourself to feed us, no need to coddle us on top of that..." Franky loved Antoinette differently. She preferred the way he loved and the image it reflected of her. My mother was a poor woman, Franky's was a bright spell in the weather. He recreated this image all the time. In fifth grade, he even won a poetry contest for Mother's Day. That was his proof. It was called "The Most Beautiful of Them All." It was chock-full of elements of style. Moved to tears, Maître Cantave said it reminded him of his childhood. Of his own mother. The eighth wonder of the world. We see people in the present moment, and we forget that even old folks like Maître Cantave and my boss, Moïse, have their own Antoinette whose image they can paint whenever they like, according to their mood or degree of talent. Even they manage to forget. Maître Cantave had forgotten. The poem roused his emotions and reawakened his Antoinette. I forget where Franky went looking for the words and images to depict a goddess. A mother full of elements of style. A supernatural creature capable of walking on water. Of course, in terms of walking, it's more beautiful and less tiresome when pavement is replaced by water. His Antoinette was every virgin all at once, every form of beauty. A kind woman and a Top Model. A tenderness. A blessing. "A miracle of love preserving the fresh scent of youth despite the passage of time." Franky knows how to write stuff like that. He always knew. Writing them, I guess, is a way to help him maintain a balance. But to believe them... Franky took many fewer beatings than I did. Because of his asthma. And the way that he took Antoinette's tales for the absolute truth. Antoinette, she had two sons. Franky was the good boy, and I was the opposite. Franky, he was the final link in the chain connecting her to her Antoine of Gommiers, and it made her proud. Even though she understood nothing about the poem. Maybe she forgot that she was "The Most Beautiful of Them All." But then again, the written word never was her strong suit. She was nothing but numbers. The count of what she carried in a white enamel-ware bowl sitting atop her head. The big bars of soap. The bottles of cheap perfume. The tubes of skin-whitening creams. On her head, all sorts of paraphernalia for miserable women looking to play perfect beauty and transform themselves into mulattoes. And inside her head, an interminable succession of losing numbers. Antoinette, she always played the numbers according to her dreams and never won. For his poem, Franky received a lunchbox as a prize. First prize in the competition. Most of the children's parents were absent during the awards ceremony. Yet, Maître Cantave went the whole nine yards. He had decorated the walls of the schoolhouse with stars cut out of colorful cardstock, suspended a few balloons from the ceiling, and prepared snacks. And he wrote a beautiful speech. It was as grand as he could muster. The few students present had taken down the stars so that they could take home with them a little sliver of the sky. The adults and children ran for the snacks. Antoinette, the laurate's mother, only managed to secure a half a slice of chicken pâté and a cup of Couronne Cola, thanks to the clever Danilo. Merci, kolonn. Unflappable, Maître Cantave finished his speech by saying, "And so writers are born." Writer, historian, to me it's all the same. If there is a difference, the only choice is in the hogwash you use to produce whatever you write. Franky spends his time navigating between the two. In History, you make choices that, later, folks will blow out of proportion, and there you are: a monster or a hero. In liteature, you make up a fable that relates to nothing at all, and we reward you for being mistaken about what's real or not. Even when your reward isn't much more than encouragement, a poor excuse for a party, and a handshake accompanied by a lunchbox that you cannot even afford to fill.

Regarding the length and the conditions of the voyage, *the editor-in-chief and owner-publisher of* "Ad Libitum", *often accused of exaggeration and partiality by his enemies and detractors, however, had not told a lie. Traveling from Port-au-Prince, the road to the master was long. Parked at the South station, the bus awaited its passengers, the most hurried of which set out as soon as the cathedral bells announced the four o'clock mass, ensuring that they would find a good seat on the bus. "Port-au-Prince, land of debauchery and lies," wrote the editorialist. It had been known for these travelers to have crossed the paths of drunkards after spending the whole night shooting dice and drinking in the bars at the gate to Léogâne, which produced troubadours whose repertoires consisted of salacious songs. The ladies, worried about being approached by the drunkards confusing them for prostitutes returning home from work and potentially available for a final go 'round, covered themselves with veils, thumbed their rosaries, or sang hymns to Our Lady of the Rosary and to Saint Christopher,* *the patron saint of travelers. The most prudish and precious ladies made sure they were accompanied from their house to the station by children living in domestic servitude who carried their effects for them. Girls angry to have been woken up earlier than normal, but happy to have the chance at a little sense of solitude, wandered in the morning's early hours, gaily musing on the road back to their chores and aprons. The bus was filled with the light of dawn and left more or less at the same time, with the rising sun. The editor-in-chief and owner-publisher of "Ad Libitum" did not embellish a thing. The route was comprised of a myriad of bumps and potholes.* Griffonnes *and* Jérémiades, *a pair of buses from each company, were winded by the ascents, out of control on the descents, one took the lead, caught up to the other, stopped, labored (oh it's so hard!), took off again (no pain, no gain!), gathered speed, lost the lead by running into an obstacle, held out hope, lost it again by running into a new obstacle, and grumbled to a halt followed by the voice of the driver who ordered: "Everyone off the bus!" The breakdown competition between* Griffonnes *and* Jérémiades *never amused the passengers. With each breakdown, a minimum of three per voyage, everyone had to step off the bus, taking along with them their most precious belongings. The most clairvoyant of ladies made sure to equip themselves with a folding chair, as well as a fan and a parasol for the waiting periods. Each driver was accompanied by a mechanic who inspired little confidence and who only understood the rudimentary aspects of his profession. In fact, they were the parents, cousins, or nephews, or even the coddled children of the drivers who lied about their competencies in order to get them hired so they could enjoy the conversation* with a relative during the trip. Among the passengers, burly volunteers and amateur mechanics took charge, making the effort to change tires, mend a leaky radiator or revive the engine. Smaller patrons, more clerks than manual laborers, took off their vests and shirts to join hands with the burly passengers, bringing them assistance more cumbersome than useful, the goal of which was to get the blood flowing in their arms and perhaps attract the attention of a certain lady open to a chance encounter. These forced breaks offered an occasion to chat, and gallant passengers also equipped themselves with stools, parasols, and fans that they offered to the lady of their choice, thus finding a way of engaging them in conversation. The hum of the tired engine and the sudden rising of dust announced the passing of a vehicle and the women rose from their seats to distance themselves from the road. The driver for the rival bus company, appearing to sympathize with the enemy driver, slowed down and waved, thus enabling his passengers to launch a few verbal jabs at the passengers of the broken-down bus. The ladies were most frequently targeted: plump ladies sweating like pigs despite their little parasols and fans; young ladies fleeing the north and the west, heading south where the men were supposedly more gullible and ready for all sorts of madness for a stuck-up, plump Madame... The men also received their fair share of insults and jeers: the men with stocky arms were called gorillas; it was said of the smaller men that their sexual attributes must be suspect if they were to be judged based on their flat torsos or the appearance and size of their forearms, skinny and shrunken like the remnants of a candlestick. Those being mocked did not anger. Without having any expertise in the calculation of probability, they knew that each bus's turn would come, and it would soon be the lot of those *doing the mocking to sit cross-legged on the side of the road and combine their efforts to get their bus started again. The time would come to return the insults and thumb their noses. In terms of victories, the* Belle Griffonne's *and the* Jérémiade's *buses arrived at their destination more or less at the same time. The seasoned travelers, traveling salesmen, and public sector employees, did not base their decision between* Griffonne *and* Jérémiade *buses on the quickness of travel or on the comfort of the interior, all things being equal. The real competition depended on which bus possessed, hidden among its riders, the best inventors of insults. The owners of the two companies, Alexandre Pinson and Auguste Pinson, two cousins with opposing manners and temperaments, hired joke specialists, genius inventors of explosive language. Their recruiting agents hung out in public places throughout Jérémie —the markets, the street corners where drunkards shout at one another, funeral processions, the wasteland where, during soccer matches, the Mayor's office set up chairs borrowed from the Presbyterian school for grandstands, the arenas housing cockfights—to scout out the ironical aesthetes and jokesters and to offer them work. The quarrel between the Pinsons dated back to their childhood, to the day when their cousin Victoria arrived from the capital one July morning to spend the summer vacation in Jérémie. The responsibility fell on them to introduce this beautiful nine-year-old stranger to the charms of the countryside and provincial life. They fell victim to her charm instead, fighting with each other like two cocks, hurting their fingers and knees to introduce their visitor to rock climbing, nearly drowning themselves in the currents of Point-à-Bec while playing master of the waters. After her departure at the end of the summer, they wrote her impassioned letters to* which she never replied. She never came back. Her parents had judged the travel conditions too horrible for a girl of the capital. Auguste and Alexandre continued to bicker with each other, they threw themselves into business, they created their own mass transit companies, secretly feeding dreams of seeing Victoria, the photos of whom indicated that she had grown to be beautiful, step down from a Belle Griffonne or Jeremiad bus. The quarrel between the Pinsons went on for no less than thirty years, while Victoria had long since been married to a French petty officer who was welcomed like a prince in the salons of the capital. On the eve of old age, the competing cousins went back to the master. Which, Auguste or Alexandre, would be able to boast of the final victory? The legend tells us that Antoine of Gommiers only accorded them a few minutes of his time, enough to predict bankruptcy and reconciliation. If you shared a first name with an emperor and had a bird's name on top of that, you might lack a little sense, too. "Long Live Diversity!" Was the way Antoine put it, since a company created by entrepreneurs in Port-au-Prince, equipped with new buses and wealthy investors connected to the Ministry of Public Transportation, established a monopoly, bringing the cousins back together by destroying their businesses. On a somber street in Jérémie, they opened a spot in one of the little houses that offered seaside views and stank of desiccated fish. The Victoria was hardly a profitable business, a bar with four tables whose clientele was made of penniless intellectuals and retired folks. They lived out old age waiting tables themselves and playing rounds of checkers with the clientele, generously ceding victory to their adversaries.

One day, Antoinette's legs gave out. She fell to the ground as she crossed Grand Rue, scattering her wares all throughout the street. Perfumes. Soaps. Barrettes. Pins. Skin-whitening creams. The entire little world of feminine products she carried on her head. Danilo came looking for me at the bòlèt bank. By the time I made it to the place where she fell, tap taps were still zig-zagging to avoid running over her body. Children were fighting with one another to pick up what was left of her merchandise. The adults had already taken the essentials. She was lying on her side, and when I turned her over. I noticed that her face had ceased to reflect the unspoken silence she carried with her every day. I no longer saw any pain. Death provided another way of seeing her. I prefer the way she looks now. She's an empty shell. She could become anything. To see things this way, you have to make some choices. In death, I chose to imagine her as close as possible to the Antoinette in Franky's poem. While they're alive, we love folks for who they are. They're right there. You don't have to make believe, it's their presence you grow to love. But, as soon as they're dead and gone, you have to give them another meaning. Something else, or something that makes them different. Maybe for Franky she was already dead, even when we heard her on the other side of the curtain, rustling in her sleep. Perhaps that's why he saw her with a blue aura, with even more beautiful attributes than in real life. Antoinette loved Franky so much you'd think that she'd choose to reside in his memories the way that he had always dreamed of her, and so to avoid disappointing him, she began to resemble the lady in the poem. Franky wanted her to be beautiful, and so she became beautiful. Franky, he was her favorite. Antoinette was a poor little woman with tired legs and two sons, one a fighter and the other an asthmatic, one of whom she preferred. Or, perhaps I'm the one who made this up. This story of post-mortem beauty. Because sometimes I daydream, too. Last night, Antoinette dreamed of a bird flapping its wings into infinity. The word for "infinity" doesn't exist in the Tchala, the book of numerology. And the wise say that its number is zero. To dream about infinity, is to dream of going too far. Or, of going nowhere at all. Antoinette fell without having enough time to place her bet or run into a hot streak. Along with Danilo, we hailed a tap tap and took her body to the Hôtel de Dieu morgue, whose owner was in debt with Moïse. Nobody suggested I call a justice of the peace to prepare the death certificate. I would've had to wait around all day. The justices don't exactly hurry over to our neighborhood. I had prepared her death certificate myself for some time now. One step at a time, just like Maître Cantave would say. Antoinette quickly progressed from a state of living-dead to dead, just like that. If I left her lying in the street waiting too long for a justice of the peace, she would quickly transform into a cadaver. A piece of material exposed for vagaries and viewing. Also, how much would the justice have charged for making the trip? Judges are expensive. And it never spells anything good when you get the State caught up in your affairs. Here, when the State finally realizes you exist it's more bad than good. The only thing that interests the state is what it can take from you. The attachés to the Mayor's office rough up the market women in their stalls only to resell the stolen merchandise on the black market. The inspectors from the Tax Assessor's office who write some random number on your tax slip and ask you to set some money aside for them, claiming they did you a favor by writing in a smaller amount than you actually owe. The traffic cops who threaten tap tap drivers with tickets unless you give them enough money to buy them a shot of rum. There's no need for a judge to fill out her death certificate. Judges, social workers, public health workers, they should've come around before.

Besides the normal stoppages, turns where the road transformed into a path inundated with cows moseying about, places where trees had fallen from the top of a hill to nestle itself across the road below, the rivers remained the worst obstacles of all. Whether flowing or desiccated, the rivers forced the bus to slow down or stop. "Ah, the rivers!" On the subject, the editor-in-chief and owner-publisher of "Ad Libitum" had broken with his well-researched, prosaic tendencies and, for "poetic purposes" opted for a comparative route: "A decrepit bus is no sailboat, and even sailboats avoid the violence of restless waters eager to set out for the high seas. A bus also is no chariot, and when rivers run dry, their beds are made of rocks too sharp for the tires, and you must zig-zag to avoid blowouts."

Departure at daybreak and arrival in Jérémie by nightfall. Soaked, dried up, and worn out. Those who came to see the master must wait till the following morning, then must take the same road in the opposite direction, until the Plain *of Gommiers. They slept, according to their means, in bed and breakfasts, pitiful dormitories, or in one of the two hotels registered with the Ministry of Tourism. They woke up early and went backward toward Gommiers on the backs of donkeys or crammed into a tap tap transporting more passengers than a clown car headed to a circus.*

Elites, government dignitaries, and foreigners traveled under more comfortable conditions, in vehicles conforming more closely to their status and fortune. Hot rods and cars with government or embassy issued license plates passed the buses, spraying dust all over the passengers seated alongside the road, the market women selling vegetables, and the cattle ranchers. Certain visitors took the liberty of showing up to the master's house with guides or their domestic servants in tow. A Syrian merchant residing in Pétion-Ville. The patriarch of a mulatto family whose business was in shambles. A minister or a managing director. A senator's wife, or the senator himself. A wealthy landowner looking to augment the yield of coffee or sugarcane production... According to a peasant claiming to be the son of the first secretary to Antoine of Gommiers, the names and dates of each visitor were recorded in a registry that had mysteriously disappeared on the very day the master passed on. Also inscribed in its pages were the names of a few American politicians, electoral candidates, as well as the names of many Hollywood stars and famous jazz musicians who were hardly satisfied with the Vodou priestesses of New Orleans. Another peasant, presenting himself as the son of the master's second secretary, denied the existence of such a registry. Antoine did not simply predict the future. He also boasted a fabulous memory and needed neither notes, nor a registry to recall dates, events, or people's names. The son of the first secretary insisted. As a humble disciple of Antoine, his father would never tell a lie. Possessing a proficiency in English, he had even served as a translator for the American movie stars. After every session, the master ordered him to place the registry in a mahogany chest in the room of treasures to which the second secretary was not permitted access. In this room said to be full of treasure, Antoine preserved precious objects offered to him by his visitors: portraits autographed by the artist, canes, statuettes, mirrors, necklaces, jewelry boxes, medals, swords, rugs, vases... Beautiful pieces that, shortly before his death, the master had appraised by a jeweler and an antiquarian sent from the capital at his request. The two experts stayed at Antoine's estate in Gommiers for five days, the antiquarian sported a three-piece suit and the jeweler a hat and a cane. During the day, they locked themselves away in the room of treasures and only left but once, at lunchtime, to get the blood flowing in their legs and for sustenance. At night, they had access to every inch of the estate, but since they were not exactly the walking type, they preferred to sit down in their rockers underneath a tree and take in the breeze while conversing about people's fascination for gold, the source of so much misery and success, and the resilience of the past in objects like a dagger, a mirror, or a bedrest. Glory and love, the twin motors of history. The jeweler fell in love with the young peasant woman who served them their afternoon meal. He made advances at her in florid French, punctuated with Latin sayings. She took pleasure in the game. He went out at night without his hat and cane, disguised as a peasant, to go join her in the shadows of the gum trees. The young woman replied to his advances by allowing him to caress her breasts and her thighs, but never her genitals. Giggling, she reminded him that there was no need for hiding places or disguises because the master knows everything—everything that had once been, everything that would, and would not, come to pass. So long as the affair never amounted to more than a few furtive caresses of her breasts and thighs, the master gave his consent. Without ever having studied the humanities or the properties of metal, the master was a true savant. He understood that in life we all need small pleasures and never intervened in ordinary affairs. Once their mission was complete, the men of the arts returned to the capital. The antiquarian left aboard a Belle Griffonne *bus, quite content to resume his routines; the jeweler took a worn-out* Jeremiade *bus, sad to return to his family life where he would long for the taste of the young woman and sapodillas. From the moment they stepped on their respective vehicles, they lost their ability to speak, only to find it again once they stepped into their homes the following day. They understood the lesson and preserved the silence about the results of the appraisal to the death. Sometimes evil can serve the cause of good. The jeweler, married to a dragon who continuously overburdened him with her disapproval, and the father to two vain and vapid daughters, pretended to be mute for two more weeks so as to not respond to his spitfire wife or the tantrums of his progeny. Silent and melancholic, he devoted his time to reading romantic and pastoral poetry inspiring daydreams, endlessly transporting him back to Gommiers, back to the virginal beauty of the young peasant woman whose breasts and thighs were all he caressed. The antiquarian was a single man more interested in his handsome apprentices to whom he introduced his profession than the female sex, lacking the audacity to act upon this ancient desire; he really had nobody else to talk to, apart from his cat, with whom he only discussed matters that had ripened for at least twenty years.*

The favorite son sat in on a talk given by a star professor, the President of the Historical Society. The President has a weekly radio program every Sunday morning where he explains all the hows and whys of great historical events. Luckily, his Sunday show isn't broadcast on Métro-Machin. Métro-Machin is all pursed lips and strait-laced. The word "folks" is forbidden on their airwaves. One time, Franky wanted to try it out, only because the President of the Historical Society granted them an interview. The radio host rolled his 'r's so distinctly, you would've thought someone stuck a shaft of wheat where the sun don't shine, and he concluded that poverty was nothing but the poor people's fault. Right you are, Mr. Radiohost! And the alleyways are dying.... Apart from Métro-Machin and the two or three other radio stations that pretend we don't exist, in the alleyways, the competition is stiff. One station per tiny room. Sometimes two. It's the war of the transistors. The only moment of the day when everyone's windows are open.

In the alleyway on Sunday morning, it stinks less outside than the other days of the week. Misery sets in when the stench activates and spreads its odors. With sweat, rotten produce, and remnants spilling out of old, perforated sacks. Sunday morning is misery's day of rest. For poor folks, rest amounts to boredom. So, to amuse themselves, everyone listens to the radio. And it makes for a hell of a show. The sermons from the evangelists awaiting the apocalypse. The programs featuring dedications of old French songs, like "Parlez-moi d'amour" for Joëlle celebrating her fifteenth birthday, from a secret admirer; or "Acropolis Adieu" for little Agathe as she's carried to the baptismal font, from her godfather. The broadcasts of Catholic mass. The President's little stories. The obituaries, accompanied by music that sounds like it's being played by ghosts. Old Spanish boleros. All these sounds devour each other all at once. And Danilo, who doesn't like Sunday because it's a day where there's no money to be made, he'll come out of his little room and shout that if folks don't turn down their motherfucking radios, he'll make sure that everyone knows the sexual exploits of every woman in the alleyway. These women don't really have many secrets in their sex lives. There aren't too many places to hide secrets. But men are suspicious, and rumors about sex, even when they're not true, cause problems, useless scandals, and folks start insulting everyone else.

The President's voice is like a pinprick, a reminder. If you didn't realize when you woke up that it was Independence Day or Flag Day, the anniversary of an important battle or treaty, all you needed was his voice to make you feel guilty for the sin of forgetting. We don't have TV, and I've never seen the President before. But I recognized his voice. A beautiful voice, like Maître Cantave. With a better vocabulary. More culture. More dates and explanations. In the alleyway, Maître Cantave, he was our knowledge, our culture. But I suppose that culture differs from neighborhood to neighborhood. There are great teachers and average teachers. Our champion, he wasn't the greatest and he didn't draw much of a crowd. His audience was full of kids whose hearts and minds were busy with other things. The President of the Historical Society had the reputation and the "aura" of a great teacher. The day Antoinette died, Franky, who only had his high school diploma, had gone to hear the President give a talk officially reserved for university students and specialists. I had a vague idea where it was. Danilo wanted to come along with me, but I preferred to go alone. I walked for a while in a part of the city I wasn't familiar with. After an hour, I managed to find it. The Society of History and Geography. The paint wasn't exactly fresh, but the building was tidy. A bay of windows with offices, and an auditorium. On the door, a sign read: *Presidential Address: "The Fragility of Oral History."* The auditorium was packed. The past has plenty of disciples. And a great teacher never speaks into a void. The entire audience was taking notes. The President's body hardly resembled his voice. His voice had presence—full of references and certainty. His body was worn out. A carcass, and not much else. The President was a star in decline. He must have had legs as tired as Antoinette's. For the same reasons. His legs must have been swollen from not moving around enough. There are folks where all you have to do is look at them for a second to figure out their preferred position. Mathilde, from the alleyway, she was born laying down. When her man, Mathias, leaves in the morning for who knows what kind of odd job, she's laying in bed on their forged iron frame. When he comes back home, he finds her still lying there. And at night, when they have sex and make noises capable of awakening the dead, she's still lying there, listening to Mathias scream "Move a little at least! " She only gets up around eleven o'clock to make the evening meal. And her expression reflects all the misery in the world. She complains about the beans that take too long to cook and, once her task is complete, she quickly goes back to lying down. For the President of the Historical Society, sitting in front of an audience is his pleasure. I heard "my thesis" so many times in the space of a minute. An old man with one or two theses, a firm tone of voice, lively eyes, and shaky hands. A scrawny man, no real stature, up to his neck in wrinkles. Yet there was a light in his eyes that shone with passion. A body full of contradictions could still explain rather dissimilar things. As though each of his body parts belonged to a different century, had lives all their own and never bothered to get caught up in one another's business. I kind of pushed my way through the admirers standing in the back of the room. When a teacher speaks, I suppose it's fair to assume that he expects to have the monopoly on making noise. The shuffling drew the attention of the great dean of yester-year. He raised his head, stopped talking, and looked at me for some time before continuing to develop his thesis. My thesis was this: Franky looked more frustrated than surprised to see me. Not because he was angry at me—we're not like that. I'm down-to-earth and he's asthmatic, but we're never ashamed of one another. My presence meant that reality had fucking come a-knocking, a problem in the present tense was calling him—some fucking emergency. I pushed my way back through the crowd of admirers to exit the room. The President continued to develop his thesis. Franky came to find me outside. He was still holding his notebook in his hand: "Alright kolonn, let's make it quick. The old woman, she dropped dead in the street." "A hit-and-run? An accident?" I would've preferred the same. The only way to avenge the dead is to find yourself an enemy to blame, someone living to fight against. With Danilo's help, we would've beaten the shit out of the bastard. We wouldn't have killed him because we're not killers. And, in order to kill him, we would've needed to get permission from Pépé or another rival gang. In the neighborhood, you can't kill someone freely. The ability to kill someone is the highest honor, it's carried out like a privilege. And if you want to be promoted to a higher rank, it's best to have the bosses backing you up. Pépé had caught some flack after Maître Cantave's murder. The bosses criticized him for going it alone. And, what's more, for killing an old man who was already part dead, only living his life in the past tense. At first, Pépé bowed his head in response, as though he accepted the sanction. Pépé wasn't a talented student of history or rhetoric, but he also wasn't stupid. Then he built up support and killed one of the bosses so that no one ever bothered to fuck with him again. We didn't have an enemy to beat up to avenge Antoinette. "No, she fell all by herself. If she didn't, then she died standing on her own two feet, and death is what brought her down." "How are we going to manage? I mean, for the funeral, the viewing, and everything else?" "Don't worry about it, I already worked it out with Moïse. And if that isn't enough, I'll talk with Danilo about whose doors we can knock on." "And what about me, how can I help?" In the meantime, the President finished developing his thesis. After the rounds of applause, the students began to open their mouths, full of questions and comments. Those who understood nothing at all, those who understood every word, those who agreed with one aspect of his thesis, but not another. For folks with time on their hands, a thesis is like a cake that you slice into many pieces, then you endlessly discuss who has the best one. There were also those who had nothing to say. Perhaps fate had brought them here into this auditorium. Or a friend dragged them there. A small group of aficionados gathered around the President. He kept talking to them as he walked towards his vehicle. A massive car, too big for his scrawny body and frame. I said to myself that he must feel pretty good, sitting alone in such a car. But the students climbed in with him. Pushing at one another to find a seat. As he drove past us with the window rolled down, he stuck out his hand to wave goodbye. He must be the kind of person used to waving at crowds of people. A gentle man. The kind of teacher to give a history lesson behind the wheel, altering his route to drop off students before making his way home. A Maître Cantave with even more knowledge and resources, with a whole group of Frankys to help him feel alive. "And what about me, what should I do?" "You, my dear brother, you weren't born to handle concrete things. Your goddess walked on water, then she fell flat on the pavement along Grand Rue. Her bowl bounced onto the sidewalk and, taking advantage of the moment of confusion, someone took it. The contents of the bowl spilled out into the street, and women came running to grab free skin-whitening creams and tablets we sometimes give to pigs to combat the excessive buildup of fat. It's on me to find the money, since the old woman left nothing behind." It's been our pact since childhood to avoid saying words that cause us harm. Franky, you're lazy. Ti Tony, you're crass. It wouldn't have helped. We're just two brothers who never bothered to fight with one another. Even when she was alive, Antoinette wasn't a reason for a power struggle. Franky, you're lazy. Loving her in the heavens, shrouded in blues. Ti Tony, you're coarse. Loving her on earth, robed in black. And that's just who we are, that's it! Franky cried in silence. I don't like to see Franky cry. His tears are sacred, that was one of the few things Antoinette and I agreed upon. For her, if he cried, everyone was at fault. Me first, then everyone else. For me, he was like this other part of myself, wounded, that I must have betrayed. So, I told him, as a way of speaking his language and sharing in his grief: "Kolonn, you take care of the words, so that way her viewing will be the most beautiful of them all."

The other half of the visitors arrived in Jérémie by way of the sea*.* *The passage differed from one boat to the other, having plenty in store to discourage the foreigners—no cabins on board, everyone on the bridge. The boat sailed the coast overloaded with passengers and merchandise, only venturing out on the high seas when necessary for a brief portion of the voyage. The crossing was still more comfortable than the bus trip. But the memory of a shipwreck leaving thirty or so dead at the beginning of the century had left its mark on the minds of the people. And the slightest bit of wind that shook the sails or caused the boat to pitch roused fear and stirred up seasickness in the most fragile passengers. The ship-owners employed children to load and unload the vessels, and they avenged themselves when faced with the arrogant adults from the capital and abroad who treated them like porters, and barked at them to be careful with the contents of the suitcases and baggage that they lugged around for a few cents. The children waited for the wind to pick up, they then walked over to the wealthiest,* *most stuck-up passengers and told them stories of shipwrecks to draw their attention. Then, they told them how the fresh air and the birds flocking to the shores announced an oncoming storm. The boat would sink. The rumors spread quickly, causing people to faint and provoking panic attacks. Assailed with questions, and hardly amused by the game being played, the captain doubled the orders to the members of the crew to re-establish the calm onboard and to punish those cursed rascals. The rascals, grinning ear-to-ear, threw themselves overboard and accompanied the boat, swimming all the way into port where they resumed their jobs as porters.*

As for the viewing, we nailed it. In addition to the humble residents of the alleyway, there were a few notable guests and enough hors d'oeuvres, alcohol, and tea for everyone, and even some akra and marinad. Moïse came by and his bòlèt bank contributed to the affair. Antoinette had been one of their regulars and one of their first clients. Moïse was still a young man when he opened his bank. In terms of the local lottery, clients don't really trust youngsters. I say it every time Moïse has to go out and leaves me by myself. Even the folks who've known me my whole life hesitate before making their purchase, almost as though they thought I would run off with their money. Antoinette trusted Moïse. I don't recall her ever not playing, it was convenient. The bank was right at the end of the alley. If you had to throw your money away, you needn't go far. When we were little, Franky wrote down the numbers Antoinette dictated on a piece of paper. I accompanied her to the bank. She played twice a week, combining all the numbers, hoping to win the

three drawings. She believed in her dreams. I wonder if she
didn't play just to have a reason to dream. There were rivers,
deaths, extraordinary circumstances, places she hadn't been
to, planes, a grand party in a palace. Invisible powers gave
her a reason to believe. In her dreams, she wasn't as sharp
and didn't understand everything. So, in another dream,
Grandma Hortense showed up in support, disguised as
a wood pigeon or a butterfly, and presented her with the
keys to interpreting the previous dream. Antoinette consulted with a self-proclaimed expert in numerology who
lived alone in another alleyway. With women, he didn't just
want to read them their numbers. He wanted them to come
alone and stay with him, moving from the living room into
the bedroom. I accompanied Antoinette and that bothered
him. He shot me mean looks and told parables about the
misfortunes that befall children who meddle with adults.
And, his house smelled terrible, and so did he. In the alleyway, you wouldn't exactly say that the houses smelled like
French perfume. There aren't enough sticks of incense or
scented candles to chase away the stench of poverty. Misery
manages to produce a kind of natural odor. The ordinary
smell of depravity, of the remnants of everyday life abandoned at the entrance to the alleyway. The 'Expert's house
reeked of a deliberate activity, of an intention. Something
intentionally stifling, like a suffocating trap, a strategy to
provoke fear. I couldn't give a damn about his parables.
Antoinette's dreams, her morning dews, her roses, and miracle birds, they cost her a pretty penny and enabled her to
confront the alarm clock. That was the only promise of the
dawn. Antoine of Gommiers was her retroactive Father

Christmas. A legend from the past who helped her appreciate life, or simply to bear it. To give her a sufficient response
to the avalanche of "why me's" capable of sending her into
despair, enough to keep her alive. Antoine of Gommiers
was her protection against the overflowing of this word,
"why." There was nothing I could do about it. But two char-
latans, that was a little too much. The second one was still
alive, with his ringed fingers, his house full of rotten smells.

One evening, Danilo and I went looking for him as
he was walking home, with rocks in our hands. My throw
missed him. He turned around and I thought he recognized
me. Danilo is a better shot. He hit the numbers man in the
tibia. I don't know if it broke the bone or not. But the next
day, when Antoinette and I arrived at his house, he wasn't
in the mood to deliver the secrets of the numbers, nor to
seduce a woman. On the way back home, I asked Antoinette
if it was normal for a descendant of the great Antoine of
Gommiers to go consult a so-called expert basking in foul
odors. I did it to mess with her. I had emphasized the words
"great" and "descendant" and I was ready to get smacked.
But she was happy that for once I spoke well of Antoine of
Gommiers. She never went back to see the expert. He kept
pursuing her, like a predator out for his prey. One morning,
he was surprised to see who was waiting at the entrance to
the alleyway. Danilo and I found some rocks, and I told him
that the next time we wouldn't aim for his legs, but this time
his head. "You understand what I'm saying? Parable for parable, prediction for prediction, or threat for threat, if you
continue in the error of your ways..." These were just words
to scare him away. In the afternoon, the ladies next door

reported the incident to Antoinette. A child doesn't throw stones or threaten adults, even if the cause is just. The old woman didn't scold me. Not even a smack or a reproach. God, could she be naive, she thought that I believed in him, in her Antoine of Gommiers. That was the only time I ever experienced the part of her that felt like respect or trust. I'm not saying that I'm jealous of Franky. Okay, maybe I'm a little more jealous than I'm willing to admit.

The visitors arriving in Jérémie by way of the sea also had to wait until the next day to make the trip to Gommiers where, according to the peasant having presented himself as the son of the first secretary to the master, Antoine Pinto, also known as Antoine of Gommiers, awaited them in his melon-colored hat and white suit, sitting in his rocker, already knowing their names and the motivations for their visit. The supposed son of the second secretary continued. Antoine did not keep a registry and what the supposed son of the first secretary called the room of treasures was really nothing more than a modest workspace, a tiny room separated from the main house. In this room whose surface area was no more than thirty-two square feet, there was only a mural of Saint Jacques the General in Ogou Fèray's clothing painted on the wall and a trunk containing all the necessary elements for certain auspices: candles, scarves, saucers, bottles containing mixtures prepared by the master, a carafe of fresh water, a small iron bed covered in a white sheet for the rare instances of possession or mental *breakdowns necessitating restraint. Totally indifferent to material things, the master refused objects of great value, just as he refused to be paid in foreign currency—he was happy with a fixed amount, seventy-seven goud, making no distinction between the rich and the poor, Black, White, mulatto, man, or woman. What the supposed son of the first secretary had presented as an estate only really consisted of a tiny property, an ordinary lakou dedicated to the cultivation of sweet potatoes and manioc, bordered in the front by a hedge of candelabra and cactuses, and in the back by a few fruit-bearing trees including a soursop tree beneath which the master places his rocker after choosing leaves for his pre-siesta tea in the beginning of the afternoon. In the lakou sits the masters house, a little bigger than the rest, the workshop and the little houses inhabited by the community of simple folk belonging to the extended family of Antoine of Gommiers.*

It is from beneath this soursop tree, in the freshness of the afternoon air, with his hat perched on his chest during his nap that the most precious divinations came to him. His body shook with a slight quiver and he, whom folks had never heard swear nor raise his voice, shouting "Aw, fuck!" as his torso rose. The movement caused his hat to fall, and his yell was so powerful that it reverberated in every corner of the lakou and even beyond its boundaries. The first time that folks heard it, the little children ran away scared, or they threw themselves into their mother's arms, busy with the laundry or harvesting fruit, which caused the fruits to fall to the ground or for their faces to be covered in a mixture of soapy foam and indigo. Their mothers didn't scold them and explained to them that the master would never do them any harm, he was the protec-

tor of everyone in the lakou. This is how great men are, they manage to accomplish and understand things that are beyond us simple folk. The children did not really understand much of their mother's philosophical reflections. They were still at the age where they hadn't unlearned the process of thinking through images, and when the master dozed off beneath the soursop tree, they conjured the image of a traveler venturing into the beyond. With time, they realized that these naps were the way that Antoine of Gommiers traveled. The shouting meant that he had arrived somewhere or at a stopping point, where the action or the landscape possessed some beautiful, epic, or fatal quality.

After having shouted and looked out at the four corners of the lakou, Antoine of Gommiers picked up his hat, placed it on his chest, and went back to sleep. When he woke up, apart from a few men working in distant fields and the women still yet to return from the market, the entire lakou was seated at his feet. The master smiled at his little crowd with a grin full of sorrow or cheer, according to the tenor of the events he had to share with them. The oldest members sat down in low chairs, their bones no longer permitting them to lower themselves to the ground. The little boys sat down on the grass or on a stump. The teenagers put a sheet or a towel on the ground and sat down, cross-legged. The lakou made itself into one at the feet of their master, who would then tell them what the future held in store.

When she had doubts, because Grandma Hortense didn't come to clarify the meaning of a dream, Antoinette asked Franky to check the corresponding combinations in the Tchala she kept on the little dresser beside her bed. The night of the viewing, the memories that came to me were more about her dreams than the life she lived. As we gathered around, folks shared anecdotes. I didn't listen. I knew as much as they did, if not more, about her daily life. But her true life took place during the night. Her nights were ravishing. So many things took place at night that were incomprehensible to the day unless they were to be translated into numbers. A flower, that was eleven. Thirteen was a sad number, for when the land was barren. A death, that was fifteen. A dead body floating in stagnant water, twenty-six. So, she played fifteen and twenty-six, combining the two to avoid any risk. "I'm sure of it. Fifteen will win the first drawing, and twenty-six for the second." A source of water was twenty-one. Falling, zero nine. I'm sure that the players who showed up to her viewing had bet on fifteen and zero nine the next morning. Only that morning they had decided not to place their bets with Moïse, so they wouldn't bother me. They lost. The winning numbers that evening signified wealth and responsibility. "Aw shit, we guessed the wrong evening!" For the player, each number is a living being with a mind of its own. Even though they were chosen the night before, the numbers appear in the morning, with their tongues sticking out, mockingly, refusing to play the game. The numbers make demands. They have their own agenda. They change their minds on a whim, without ever being mistaken. The players are the ones who own up to their mistakes. "Mea culpa! Mea maxima culpa! I'm but a mere mortal, I misread the signs." Yes, for the lottery player, the numbers are the leprechauns who make fun at our expense. And, at the same time, they're the wisemen who propose riddles for us. Their messages are always coded, they love to play with secrecy. Our job is to be on our game. When Antoinette's dreams were positive, she played more aggressively. The spirits are mischievous and tell us things in reverse, and since many players lost because they failed to turn in the numbers in the proper order, she often played the "reversed numbers." Fifteen and fifty-one. Twenty-six and sixty-two. Reversed or not, she lost. In my head, I calculated the sums she lost when we arrived at the bank. I quit school very early. I was tired of it—there was all this stuff you had to pretend to learn. Antoinette scolded and smacked me because of it, just to keep up appearances. She knew, I knew, that she couldn't afford to pay for the two of us. She refused to think about it, much less to say it. To take the pressure off her, I made the final decision. Since Maître Cantave's death, we really didn't learn much at school anymore. If Franky managed to learn something, it was because he studied by himself and didn't listen to the teachers. He studied so much that he could've taught the course for the teachers. And he could've continued and become a university student. But what Antoinette earned wasn't enough for him to make it to high school. We never talked about it. One of us went looking for little odd jobs while the other continued to wear out the seat of his pants on the benches of an institution like Le Savoir where he learned nothing at all. I started looking for little odd jobs with Danilo. One day, Moïse told me to come work for him, and I said yes. That's how I started earning a little bit of the money that Antoinette and the other numbers-lovers had spent their lives losing.

The night of the viewing, Moïse was there. He was nearly an old man, still without a wife and kids, alone. He'd invested his money in a few small businesses, without anyone to share it with. This often brings him some company, when he lets his investors' money ride, and then asks the folks he helps to keep it a secret. Moïse has plenty of secrets linking him to a network of people. Pépé also came to the viewing, looking very dignified in a suit, accompanied by his bodyguard, a dude known as "Bermuda Triangle." All that Pépé managed to retain from Maître Cantave's lessons was a piece of geography, a few images of the world beyond Port-au-Prince, two place names in particular: the Windward Passage and the Bermuda Triangle. They sounded nice enough, he thought, to serve as peoples' names. The first one was already taken. Someone from the Artibonite had attempted at least seven times to make the clandestine voyage towards the coast of Florida. And all seven times the American Coast Guard had brought him back. He escaped from the detention center all seven times, too. So, the Coast Guard and guards at the detention center nicknamed him "Windward Passage." When Pépé recruited Anastase to his gang, he felt that such a name didn't really fit this colossus whose specialty was making nuisances disappear. If someone was a problem. There was no need for guns. Anastase would say, "leave him to me." And he'd sling a package over his shoulder, and the problem would disappear, mysteriously sinking to the bottom of the Bay of Port-au-Prince. Pépé nicknamed him "Bermuda Triangle." I don't know who to compare Triangle to. His body is built like a wall. When he set his mother up in the alleyway next to ours, he showed up in a tap tap, the back of which was bursting with kitchen appliances. He set her house up all by himself. The refrigerator. The kitchen table and chairs, the sofa, and the electric oven, which he blew up that very evening. He brought her another one the next day, but his mother didn't want it. For her, to possess such a machine was to flirt with the devil. So, he took it back to the store, carrying it on his back alone. Pépé says that out of all the members of his gang, Triangle is the only one who would never betray him. You don't betray the person who gave you your name. Triangle appreciated his nom de guerre more than even his role as the second in command, it fit his size and skillset well. The night of the viewing, the two of them were there. Triangle stood behind his leader. Pépé no longer really operated out of the neighborhood, but he was born in the alleyway and made it his duty to grace important events with his presence. Antoinette's death was a major event. In the alleyway, she was one of the oldest residents. She saw families arrive, one after the other, and could call each child by their first name. The "Doyenne," that was her nickname. She was one of the nobles, even more so than Pépé and Moïse. There was also Monsieur Guillaume, the director of the private school Le Savoir. A paunchy man who had replaced Maître Cantave, but only taught math and observational learning, leaving the dangerous material like history and civics to a boyish colleague whom all the girls fawned over. Who had the "Doyenne" fallen in love with? She never talked to us about our father. There was this void in our memories, a vast nothingness between Antoine of Gommiers and our lives in the alley leading to Grand Rue. It was as though all that happened between these two moments was nothing more than a succession of failed numbers, a half century of malatyonn, fake numbers meant to attract the numbers junkies, that Antoinette purged from her memory or merely kept to herself, sparing us her history of failures. The only frame of reference was this Grandma Hortense of whom she didn't even have a picture. The Doyenne hadn't kept a single trace of her past. Her room of treasures was vacant and not very spacious— a small trunk in which she had only preserved a necklace and a photograph. The photo was of Franky and me when we were little, both in our cowboy costumes, sitting on a wooden rocking horse, toy pistols in hand. At the time, we looked so much alike that it was impossible to tell one of us from the other. So she wouldn't forget which one was which, she wrote our names beneath our hats.

The Doyenne didn't have many possessions herself. A pair of flip-flops and another pair of worn-out shoes. Her Tchala and this gold necklace her Grandma Hortense gave her, which was supposedly blessed by Antoine of Gommiers. Some blessings are better than others, and we refused the one offered by the pastor of the Église de la Dernière Chance. Though, he still came to the viewing. He sat alone in his corner, with a sullen look on his face, his bible resting on his knees. When seated in public, the pastor always kept his bible resting on his knees. He sulked. In his mind, every dead person in the neighborhood had to go through him to have even the slightest chance of making it into the kingdom of heaven. Franky and I decided we'd leave God out of it, and the viewing alone would serve as a ceremony, in the alleyway. Antoinette belonged to the alleyway. Even Magdalène stayed and participated until the end. Monsieur Guillaume wanted to make a speech, for he was the brains of the alleyway. But, if to be human is to have style, he was a lesser human than his predecessor. Maître Cantave would've found the right words and would've made Antoinette the heroine of her own legend: a queen without a royal name… Maître Cantave, even when he said any old thing, would always strike the right chord. Monsieur Guillaume's rhetoric was more formulaic, rote expressions like "everything will be paid in full at the beginning of the month," or "please see the registrar before entering the classroom." He never treated students like morons. In the alleyway, Maître Cantave's death had erased the word from everyone's vocabulary, teachers, students, and parents alike. Treating anyone like a "moron" had become as dangerous as calling someone an "ugly motherfucker." Insults are kind of a sport in the alleyway. Even the person you hurl your insults at is ready to congratulate you if you land a good one. But you can never say "pigfaced motherfucker." I'm not sure why though. Franky has "a thesis." He stole this expression from the President of the Historical Society. When Franky has a thesis, it's best to get comfortable, because it could take a while. I didn't understand his thesis at all. It was too lengthy, and too detailed—a Franky original. Me, I think it's simply because pigs eat shit. As for the word "moron," there's no need for a thesis on the matter. Pépé warned that the first person who said this word would end up like Monsieur Cantave. Monsieur Guillaume obeyed. He plans to live for a long while, and all he ever wanted from students was their tuition money and to get into the young ladies' panties. The night of the viewing, he spoke as poorly as usual. His speech was terrible and Pépé motioned for him to make it quick. Danilo tried to crack a few jokes to make folks laugh and get over their sobbing. He was unsuccessful. Danilo has this ability to think up all sorts of hustles, he has many skills, but telling stories isn't one of them. Meanwhile, two more people showed up whom nobody recognized. A young man in a peasant outfit, wearing a dyakout, a straw hat, armed with a walking stick made of gayac. One might say he looked like a caricature from another century, like something you'd find on a postcard. The other guy was older. His dried-out guitar in its case. His back slightly hunched. His cadence a little nonchalant. But the expression on his face was grave. His gaze was hardened, sharp like a machete prepared to carve the enemy's flesh. Triangle, seeing the guitar case, put himself in front of his leader and the pastor, and waved at them to stop from coming closer. Franky told them to respect the silence and stood up to welcome the two men. "They're friends of ours." Triangle sat back down behind his leader once more. "A descendant of Antoine of Gommiers, the greatest oracle the country, perhaps the modern world has ever known, deserves to be recognized. I asked them to come, and they accepted. Thank you, my friends." It was a performance, just for us, in memory of Antoinette. This was the first time artists came to perform in the alleyway. The young man refused the chair we offered. His art required him to remain standing. He began, "Krik!" and in spite of ourselves we responded: "Krak!" And he started telling stories by tapping his walking stick on the ground at the beginning and the end of each story. The guitarist with the tragic looking face accompanied him in the songs that were part of the stories. And as the stories flowed, we all became children again. Stories like: 'Konpè Si, Konpè Sa'–Brother this and Brother That. 'Who went to the forest at dawn?' One about friendship and gossip called, 'Thézen, zanmi mwen Zen.' 'The fish who died lovesick.' 'The kayiman who went to the royal ball and couldn't find a suit that fit.' And 'the rivers that flowed in Antoinette's dreams.' 'An Orange Tree that never stopped growing until it reached the heavens.' And 'the man whose hat fell into the sea, dove in to recover it and never again reached the water's surface'—that'll teach you to flirt with the sirens.... And 'the brave Bouki who never ceased to be duped by his brother, Malis.' We became children once more, and with every foolish thing one of the protagonists did, the sentence came forth: "If you continue in the error of your ways..." Triangle laughed and you would've thought a building had been shaken by an earthquake. Even Magdalène lost her desire to go lie down. The pastor maintained his sour look. Undoubtedly jealous. The monopoly of souls, I guess that's what passes for the monopoly of stories. The President of the Historical Society should develop "a thesis" and give a discourse on the topic of narrative competition. But, we knew, for the pastor, that sometimes in the intimacy of his chambers, that the youngest servant girls replaced the bible on his knees. No matter how much he preached against the use of condoms, they'd become his preferred mode of contraception after rumors emerged of a pregnant adolescent "Sister in Christ," earning her a prolonged leave of absence from the church. Delivering the good word of Christ is always easier when you're playing with house money. Pépé shot the pastor a look as if to say, "Stop acting like a fool. Have fun like the rest of us." The night of the viewing, we all became children. Bravo my brother! You called on the memory of Antoine and these old popular folktales. Antoinette was no longer here to enjoy it for herself, but she certainly would've appreciated it. The storyteller made us young again. In the end, even the pastor of the Église de la Dernière Chance placed his bible on the seat of his chair to offer his applause.

When it came to the old man who accompanied the storyteller, it was something else. As he began to sing the lyrics to the songs in his repertoire, we transformed back into adults, even the children. No more sirens making love to mortals, paunchy whales or large balls of water were never mean to begin with, no more orange trees that climb to the heavens or treasure buried beneath the earth. Instead, the suffering of everyday life. Revolt. The brutal return to reality. Our lives, really. His metaphors wouldn't have been Maître Cantave's cup of tea, he hated harsh language. The songs were ugly like the truth, beautiful at the same time. A beautiful ugliness that reminded us of who we were, far from Franky's blues. It's strange how suffering cannot bring a song to its end. Some of the folks in the crowd recognized the songs and belted out the choruses. We'd come full circle over the course of a viewing. The next morning, Danilo asked me how much the performances from the night before were going to cost us. *Nothing. It was free of charge. Franky just asked, and they came.* At the same time, Danilo insisted—Franky had taken a huge risk inviting a politically active singer who was hated by gangs and the police alike. His concerts normally ended with riots. As for the student from the National School for the Arts, there was no problem with his slightly childish folktales. But the singer, his voice, his words, they're a declaration of war. *Seriously, Franky went too far.* But Pépé listened to the songs and clapped his hands along with the rest of us. With Triangle in tow, whose very stature provided a protective air, Pépé went to congratulate the singer, thanking him for speaking of the woes of the people who lived "under his protection."

Antoinette warranted her own celebrity, even if she wasn't more than a star in the eyes of lowly people and had to go underground after every one of her concerts. And so, Danilo didn't have to critique Franky. Antoinette's memory is divided into two halves: one for her down-to-earth son and the other for her asthmatic son. We each do what we choose with our part of her memory. "Hey kolonn, I was just messing with you. He did the right thing, bro. He's just not like us. He knows everyone. And the old lady, don't you think she had the right, for one evening, to greet death in peace, along with all the wonders and rage that she lacked in this life?" What was Danilo getting at? Antoinette was gone. Franky was all I had left. I wasn't going to look for reasons to critique him. Franky and I, we're not like those family members seen on TV shows, the ones who never stop bickering. Bickering over belongings or just to determine which one's more important or contributes more to the family tribe. Words can sometimes be deceptive. They only indicate your role rather than describing what you do for the family. Brother. Mother. Family. We never used words like that. Franky's my number one kolonn, my best friend. We're welded together. Not even a finger can slide between the two of us. We had no use for property or tribes. We always knew that our lone inheritance was one another. Franky's going to look elsewhere, inventing a story for ourselves. But maybe this could be a way of enhancing our way of being alone together in this world. Family, we don't really know what it means. We're two children in a photograph. We put Antoinette's necklace into the coffin with her. Two children in a photograph. Two children, without even a necklace to forge the link between themselves or anyone else.

***It was then, at the closure of his siesta one afternoon in
November,*** *that Antoine of Gommiers announced, before the
analysts, the diplomats, the spies, and the foreign correspon-
dents, the awakening of a war that would bind the continents
together by blood, opening the gates to the usage of perfected
death machines on land and by sea, which would come to an
end after the extermination of millions of innocent people. A
war whose echoes would reach us from afar, heard with a relative indifference. We ourselves would be concerned with wag-
ing a war against a terrible malady stripping the earth bald
and guzzling its elixir of life until the trees' roots dry out. Then
the waters of the heavens became for us a great danger. We are
an insignificant people, and the insignificant do not get mixed
up in the matters of the important. This war would be waged
between important people, during which they would enlist
the insignificant, and many countries would end up changing
their name or simply disappearing from the map of the world.
The war, without directly concerning us, would have a great*

impact on life and economics in our country. The war would generate popular first names like Hans and Jozef as well as the usage of family names like Himmler and Goebbels as inventive first names. The war would bring with it a shortage of imported luxury products, it would reinforce the influence of one important neighboring country that hoards all the stars for itself, it would cause the arrival of new Blan, foreigners, lost and fleeing, belonging to two separate camps, and looking for refuge in a country where being of the white race, without difference of nuance, amounted to a profession or capital.

The malady stripping the earth bald tore out the roots, and as the trees fell one after the other, all that was left on the summits of the mountains was a white, talcum-like powder, drier than the starchy substance that covered roofs in periods of drought. In the rainy season, the waters from the heavens, victorious against the powder, would come down from the mountains and would relentlessly carve out a path to the sea, destroying everything in its wake—people, their livestock, and their material possessions. In a matter of seconds, the waters would settle down in a city, surprising its inhabitants attending to their ordinary affairs, felling the flags on the public buildings, pouring into bedrooms, taking with it cradles and the babies nestled in them, breaching the walls of businesses and factories, taking clerks and workers with it, too. The raw materials and merchandise would float around for a time, and folks would have a hell of a time dredging the pond, causing the drowned bodies to breach the surface once more.

As though to respond to the fury of the heavens, the earth demanded its right to vengeance. And so, as soon as the people finished shaking themselves dry and burying their dead, eager to return to their businesses and their homes, the earth, proving that it would be wrong to assume it firm and solid, shattered beneath their feet into a thousand cracks swallowing whole buildings and the people inside, as well as the errant dogs not quick or united enough in their flight. Along with the white, talcum-like dust, drier than starch covering the mountaintops, a cloud of concrete obstructed the view. People groped their way through the city stumbling over the ruins, their eyes wounded by flecks of cement and glass. It would not be until later, when the dust had settled in the evening, that you could notice the dead bodies impaled by rebar protruding from the fallen buildings. Haggard folks walked by with an arm or a leg amputated, as though granting the earth a token piece of flesh and bone to spare them the rest of their lives. And for a long while, those who are called nothing more than "survivors" will look in vain for the site where their house once sat, for their childhood garden, for the school they attended with enthusiasm when the teacher was pretty, and with apathy and dejection when she wasn't. They'll look in vain for the bench where they first experienced love, the family courtyard in which they watched the sun rise to the cock's song. For some time, the women will mourn these promised futures transformed into memories. And their friends from far and wide will come dressed in white. True friends will melt into the crowd, blending their sweat with that of the survivors, helping them to erect a wall, patch up a wound, or knead bread. The others will add insult to injury by declaring themselves the masters of the cities and the lakou, they'll sign treaties in foreign languages, and do even more harm to the people and the earth than they were capable of doing to themselves.

Antoinette's been gone a while. We're the only ones left.

The two of us. Franky spending his days with his old books, pencils, and notebooks. Me spending mine filling out cards for the clients and getting yelled at by Moïse, who yells as a matter of principle, even though, deep down, he's a really gentle man that listens to chamber music in his slippers from his house in Bas Peu de Chose on Saturday and Sunday nights. Grand Rue and the alleyway are his adoptive country. He came from Bas Peu de Choses a long while ago, and only the extremely old folks remember there's a past that precedes his presence here, the bòlèt bank and his other businesses. His other businesses are his real source of income. The bank is just an affiliation, a branch of nothing at all, a point of sale for a centralized bank. He leaves the management of the other businesses to some really smart dudes who'd never steal from him because of his connections, and he spends his days at the bank where I could manage everything on my own. He hangs around just to see people. I think he's fond of his clients, in his own way. Whether they win or lose, he couldn't care less. Seeing them come by is the essential thing. When a client stops coming by and it's not because they're sick or they've moved, he worries and asks me if we treated them poorly the last time he had come around. When it's a death, he gets angry at death, which could've waited a little while longer: "The poor bastard only won twice." Some bosses, hustlers, and businessmen get angry when it comes time to pay. Their faces drip with disdain when they have to reach for their money. You see, if it were only up to them, it would never work out this way.

Danilo worked in a factory. The boss, Monsieur Andy or something, bemoaned payday and handed out envelopes to the workers, his crying eyes weeping behind black glasses. Moïse pays without balking. It's actually the only time you see him smile. He's a kind dude, cultivating an image of a jerk who could care less about everyone else, when in reality, he's the neighborhood benefactor. He cultivates his image to the point that he keeps on shouting at us even when the clients are ready to cut us some slack or when it's just the two of us at the bank. I hear him like a person forgetting to take off his mask as he goes to take a piss in the backyard. Afterwards, I hear him chuckling alone, having cracked himself up in some backyard that stinks of dead rats and where the only real humor involves him and his prostate. A few days after Franky came home after his accident, Moïse invited us over to his little apartment in Bas Peu de Chose, his own private place, his Saturday evening residence, his place of truth, as Antoinette would say. Franky enjoyed the chamber music. Moïse paid for our taxi ride home and as we got out of the taxi, while I was getting Franky situated in his chair, he couldn't stop talking about it, this calming music that to him sounded marvelous. To Franky, lots of things are marvelous. The past. Music. The books with tattered pages that Savior, the bookseller, brings him. Suffice it to say, these things do not come from the alleyway.

We're the only ones left.

The two of us. Franky who has trouble reaching down into the large container when he's thirsty. And me, who sometimes forgets, when I'm running late or don't have the capacity to remember all my chores, to fill a bottle and to place it on the table next to his glass before leaving for work.

The two of us. Franky, exiled in a chair whose mechanism is starting to break. I tried dismantling it, greasing its joints and bolts, and putting it back together, but the chair just won't roll. One of the gifts from the doctors at the international hospital where Franky stayed for more than a month while he underwent operations, got stitched up and unstitched. They saved his neck, but not his kidneys.

Franky tries to do things for himself and suffers from failure, from not being able to go to the latrine. And I'm ashamed of him sometimes because he's incapable of carrying out all the banal acts that constitute the unraveling of our daily lives. Afterwards, I'm ashamed of myself.

The two of us. Franky's busted gift-chair no longer responds to his commands. And I take it outside when I come home. At the end of the day, I help my boss with the accounting and organize his files. We then wash our hands with a large block of soap because we've been handling the bills and, the truth is, money is dirty. All these bills have passed from pocket to pocket, from bra to bra, from one little hustle to the next. The bills come to us after a long history of petty transactions. They carry a trace of every exchange—creased and crumpled, like the clients' faces. They've been objects of hesitation and brawls between hands greedy to grab ahold of them and hands reticent to let them go. They smell of moldy sweat. Having been tucked into panties, underwear, stockings or socks, or less frequently into a hole beneath a rotting floor. The days of mattresses and pillowcases are over. They're the first places where a husband, a wife, and children will go looking. Money, since the poor live in packs, they hide on their person. Their last resort is to hide it inside their body, somewhere where they can touch it, constantly verify its presence, and say to themselves—this is what I have left. And when it's time to pull it out of its hiding place, the time has come to use this last resort. It's the white flag of defeat. To acknowledge your nakedness in the face of what is to come. Rather than purchasing one last pinch of rice, a big loaf of bread, a little bit of sugar, understanding that it will only sustain them for a few more days, some folks come and tempt their fate at Moïse's bank.

Money, when you have so little of it, all you can hope for is that it bears fruit. And so, you go to Moïse's. You withdraw your last deposit from its hiding place, your worthless trump card. You hesitate when choosing a number. You can't play all the damn numbers. Then you resign yourself. The words stumble out of your mouth: go with twelve and sixty-two. You change your mind. No, go with fifteen and fifty-one. It's also not true about money, that it doesn't have an odor. It smells of cooking oil, charcoal, mabi or smoked herring. Sometimes sperm. And perfume, too. The right odor can carry luck as well. But they don't sell *eau des pauvres* in the boutiques frequented by the children living in paradise for whom Métro-Machin advertises. Sometimes there's nothing more to a perfume than the name. There are bills that stink, or that are so worn that we're forced to refuse them. Moïse still takes three dirty bills per day out of charity. At the end of the day, he insists—use the big bar of soap to wash it all away. Then we close the bank with two locks and an iron bar. I go retrieve the daily special that Martine, the market woman who sells hot meals, has wrapped up for us in a plastic bag. Except for Thursdays. On Thursdays the daily special is a pork ragout. On Thursdays, I order the lambi. Franky hates pork ragout. Just because he can't move on his own doesn't mean I have to force him to eat something he despises. By the time I arrive at the entrance to the alleyway, the school children have already returned, reuniting with the babies and the poorer children who spend the entire day bickering, which makes for a brood that's impossible to handle. To have some peace and to appear as though in control, the mothers have already started to beat on their children, all while holding a conversation with the neighbors about everyday life. The rise in prices. Slap. The promises of politicians. Slap.

Some woman who shouldn't have gotten back together with some man who's only going to get her pregnant and leave again. Slap. The noises on the corrugated roof at night: "If it's a wily spirit who wishes to harm my children, cross of wood, cross of iron, in the name of all the saints of paradise and all the spirits of Ginen, what he's got coming, not even Antoine of Gommiers could've predicted." One slap to protect the child from wily spirits. And a woman pretending to be pregnant even when she's not. One slap so the younger sibling doesn't follow their older sister down the path of lies. The rats have lost their minds and they no longer hide, looking you straight in the eye, immune to every poison, challenging you, "catch me if you can." Take that, two slaps for the rats. And it goes on like that for a while. There's no lack of subject matter. Or rats. Or children. Sometimes the hand misses its target. The children have learned the art of flight and escape from the rats. But they're so numerous that if you miss one, you'll hit another one. And it continues. Two slaps because you tried to run. And the children, they scream, intentionally cranking up the volume to draw attention to their situation. They tattle to protect themselves: "He's the one who started it by putting his hand in my underpants!" "No, she's the one who asked me to go out back, behind the latrines, to show me her privates!" And the boy's mother says, "that'll teach you not to stick your finger where you shouldn't!" Slap. The girl's mother says, "And when he gets you pregnant, what am I supposed to do with you and your baby?" A slap from the girl's mother. And the girl isn't quite at the age where she can get pregnant, to carry a child she'll have to wait another four or five years, but simply curious and without any other toys to play with than her body. She howls, "He only used his finger!" "Yes, his finger, while waiting for it to grow and transform into something else!" her mother replies with a preventative slap. One for later. Four or five years later, when his finger transforms into something else. And the girl howls. She received more blows than the boy. Because in the alleyway, girls' bodies are always the ones that offend. And so, a neighbor, a woman who doesn't have any children, or a husband in the house, a woman who the other women find too "modern," who sings the song of romance by night suddenly wished to play the role of the mediator, the good soul, the marital counselor. "Have mercy, sisters! They won't do it again." And the boy's mother, two slaps. His last. Not because the neighbor without any children convinced her, but because deep in her soul she's proud of her little rooster who's gotten a fresh start seducing girls. "And the little hens have to learn how to fend them off!" Two more slaps from the girl's mother, for having lashed out on purpose. Her last. Not because she didn't wish to beat her daughter anymore, but because she found another target. This madwoman who takes herself for an artist, who doesn't dress the same way we do, who sometimes has a look of contentment, laughing to herself, alone in her house—what's she doing butting in? "Fuck her desire to stand out!" Now, it's a matter between big folks; the dispute increases intensity. And the girl's mother says to the neighbor without any children, "what're you do-ing butting in? If we don't even have the right to discipline our children anymore... They're children, their wounds will heal. And besides, what's a mule like you know about children?" Some children disagree with their mothers. Their wounds heal with scar tissue, on the skin's surface and on the inside. Children have their own way of seeking vengeance, laughing through the tears as they count their wounds. Now that these women are fighting amongst themselves, perhaps they'll leave the children be.

"Same time tomorrow, in the latrines? Yes, same time tomorrow."

Without records, it is impossible to reconstruct with any detail the tenor of Antoine of Gommier's precious revelations and the multiplicity of subjects to which they pertain. *Just as it is difficult to determine what relates to the fate of individuals from that which concerns the future of entire communities. The master cultivated the mystical and left up to those listening the responsibility of reestablishing meaning about the order of things. It is possible that due to the general lack of learned knowledge among the audience, comprised mostly of illiterate and uneducated farmers, they may have confused places and eras and felt contempt toward the meanings of numerous allusions. The interpretations vary. Such a prediction could also be understood as the announcement of a great political crisis or the coming of a natural disaster. The testimonies gathered by the sons of the secretaries constitute weak, secondhand oral accounts, given the slight behavioral and linguistic tick from which the two men appeared to suffer. The peasant presenting himself as the son of the first secretary is* *a loquacious storyteller, allowing himself to get carried away with the power of words, constantly going back over the details, exponentially multiplying his interruptions and additions in an interminable sequence of digressions and clauses. One cannot therefore draw a coherent, or even definitive, interpretation from his retellings. The one who presented himself as the son of the second secretary appears more interested in playing the role of the contradicteur than in performing his own narrative; perhaps it is a sign of hereditary frustration for only occupying a secondary role. So we have not accounted for, apart from rare exceptions, the facts, remarks, and circumstances on which they could have agreed, or confirmed through other sources.*

Following his great revelations, the master remained silent for some time and never came back to life once the night had fallen, when Jeanne, the young peasant woman who served him his meals (the very woman who would've had an adventure of minor consequence with the antiquarian mentioned by the so-called son of the first secretary since it was only a matter of slight touching and feeling) brought him his favorite dish, a kalalou djondjon with white rice, leaning towards him in her low-cut camisol, her breasts in full view.

The two of us. Franky locked away in the bedroom. With his paralyzed legs, if I didn't come home one day it'd be like having his arms cut off. Sometimes I hang around deliberately, but it's rare, since I'm tired of having to be indispensable toward him. We're united in the face of adversity, we're all that each other has left. As for myself, what am I if not the public face of an old couple forged by childhood memories which have taken on the burden of a promise. I don't normally run late. Faithful to my post, I enter the alleyway. If I don't say hello to these women, the deceased Antoinette could be accused of having taught us a lesson in contempt. If I do say hello, I run the risk of being taken as a witness, summoned to give my impressions by either of these warring women. "Hold on Ti Tony, listen to me..." And her neighbor will interrupt, "No, Ti Tony, she's lying, this is what happened..." Then I'll ask them to excuse me. "Franky's all alone, I've got to go." And Franky's name introduces a lull to our interaction: "Oh, right, poor Franky."

"Poor Franky." We eat without saying so much as a word to one another. He must be exhausted by this word "poor" that always precedes his name. Throughout the day, he must hear the gossip. About the accident. About his physical state. About me, the one who works for two. The ladies sometimes bring by coffee and cookies. Some come by because though they're mean to their children, they can be gracious towards a handicapped neighbor. The others come by to spy on him. Knowledge is a weapon, and it's useful to gather information that could one day prove useful. They love to stick their nose into their neighbors' business. In the alleyway, everyone brags a little bit about the things they own so that they don't come off as the poorest neighbor. So then, we spend time looking for pretexts to enter their homes to verify what's inside. Franky and I eat in silence. Sometimes I ask him where he is in Antoine's life story. "I'm moving right along." After we eat, I'm the one who moves him along by pushing his chair. I take him for a walk in the alleyway, towards the public baths to wash up or take care of our business. If I have the energy and he's in the right mood, we go out onto Grand Rue. The adults show their compassion. The children don't poke fun. They've counted their blows and are enjoying an interlude ahead of their evening beating. In the alleyway, beatings occur in a planned sequence, at specific times, so why create a situation that would cause the violence to return early. In addition, they've received strict instructions. Everyone in the alleyway knows that Moïse is connected to Pépé, Ti Joël, the lieutenants and the gang leaders. These are the conditions that allow him to run his lottery and manage his real business. Danilo tells me that when we walk around the neighborhood like this, we look like characters in a play. Danilo went to the theater, once. To the Rex. When he was just a kid, he worked on the street advertising who knows what. Some dude walked over and invited him to the theater. A smartly dressed man in a jacket and vest. An invitation to go to the theater, you just don't turn that down. Danilo accepted without asking too many questions. I think he already knew the answers. Everyone seemed to know and respect the gentleman. He looked at Danilo with a great deal of tenderness, as though, in his clothing unsuitable for a theater outing, he looked like a spectacle. Nobody appeared too surprised to see an adult in a suit jacket accompanied by a rather dirty, near adolescent clearly lost among all these beautiful people. During the play, the gentleman didn't force anything, he was a rather timid man with an expression on his face that seemed to ask for forgiveness. There are folks like that who seek out forgiveness as an advance on future crimes. When he moved his hand towards Danilo's knee, Danilo pretended not to notice and shifted his knee further away. Taking advantage of a small group of confused theatergoers asking the man his opinion on the play, Danilo gave a "Thank you sir," and left. Danilo doesn't give a shit what you do with your penis, he just wasn't interested. He didn't fault the guy for seeing him as a one-night stand. He loved the play. It was about two homeless men walking through a city. One of them disabled, sitting in his wheelchair, and the other is well-built and pushes him around. He still talks about it to this day. About these two men, and especially about the dogs. He couldn't forget the dogs. It's got this scene, he says, they're walking through the upscale neighborhoods when they're attacked by dogs. The handicapped man falls from his chair and the well-built man fights off the dogs, using his own body to protect his friend's. The crowd cackled. The laughter, Danilo didn't understand why they were laughing. Maybe it was because they couldn't see the dogs on stage. Maybe the folks in the crowd have never had to protect a friend in the street at night—maybe they've never reached out their hand to ask for help. The gentleman was one of few who didn't laugh. A man who looks to pick up kids off the street must know that dogs, when they come together in a pack, if you're alone and defenseless, they'll attack. Danilo has also been homeless. He saw them, the dogs, and he had the desire to fight alongside the well-built man. Danilo, he always wants to fight. The important thing is that he noticed the dogs while the other spectators, those who paid for their seats, didn't notice the dogs at all or the two guys they were surrounding. The play was called *Kavalye pòlka*. And the characters were named Fatal and Loréal. Where did the author come up with a name like that? Fatal, what a foreboding name. Danilo doesn't believe in fate, but he saw the whole thing, the two guys never abandoned one another, one wouldn't go anywhere without the other. And the dogs kept circling. Except around here, the dogs surrounding us are humans like us. In the alleyway, we're the dogs, cast out just like they are, without a future or a provenance. And in our pack, Franky and I are the kavalye pòlka, the bohemian cavaliers. I'm my brother's Fatal. We're the two dogs who form a pair. Franky has enough style for the both of us, and I push him around in his wheelchair.

Afterwards, we go back home. He goes back to Antoine's life. And I stick around outside to smoke a cigarette, the only one of the day. I raise my head to watch the smoke waft upward, never reaching the sky. Some evenings, even though I raise my head, you wouldn't believe there was a sky above. A black mass of which we are nothing but the foundation. Then I go inside to lie down. Franky snores. He's a dreamer who snores. I look at his legs that are now nothing more than a memory. I fall asleep, my arms heavy from having pushed his chair. I never remember my dreams. Antoinette, she did all she could to teach me how to find comfort in the world of legends and prophecies. But I never could learn. Danilo always tries to get me involved in some racket or in one of his crazy ideas, always doomed to fail. I turn him down and he says, "Kolonn, it's crazy how hard-headed you can be." That must be it. Some dogs are just hard-headed.

*One cannot begin to tally the number of people who visit-
ed the master,* nor the anxieties and hopes that drove them
to Gommiers. The editor-in-chief and owner-publisher of the
periodical "Ad Libitum" had written in one of his editorials
that in addition to his legendary incompetence, the Minister of Public Works must have had ulterior motives for leaving National Route Two, a more heavily traveled road than
Route One leading north, in such miserable disrepair. "Did
he wish to cast doubts on the political establishment and
provoke a political crisis? Did he wish to cause the School of
Engineering, where he served as the associate dean before his
entrance into politics, to close? Did he wish to contribute to
a thinning of the population by multiplying the number of fatal accidents? Will a seer grant us the keys to this mystery?"
The allusion was clear. In his youth, the Minister, a Southern man and a follower of the chronicler, had called on the
Great Antoine once on the way to Port-au-Prince and fortune
smiled upon him. Cut to the quick, the Minister had asked

the President for a dispensation of a week to respond to this piddly, fifteen-line article in a periodical that counted no more than thirty or so subscribers. The Minister's reply, written by his chief of staff, a member of the literati delighted to write something other than memos, multiplied the number of adjectives he used in defense of the idea that, he "a Cartesian, a reader of Voltaire, a logical rationalist, a Christian Scientist and researcher," had ever set foot in the home of any such seer. In closing, he highlighted the steps the entire government and his department, in particular, continued to improve the state of the national highways and put the nation on guard against "the slander dictated by failure and bitterness, as well as the nefarious effects of superstitious practices." There was no proof that National Route Two was more travelled and more deadly than the northern route. The only grain of truth in the polemic between the Minister and the chronicler pertained to two concurrent practices concerning the visitation of Antoine of Gommier's ounfò: accusation and denial. Many were the brothers, neighbors, former classmates, rejected lovers, the priests dreaming of becoming a bishop who cast suspicion on the successes of a competitor or an enemy who, according to them, lacked the personal merits. Success could not only come to someone through the assistance provided by the master in exchange for God-only-knows what wagers or sacrifices. The accused could suffer from being placed under quarantine, which closed to them the doors to mundane clubs and salons, the halls of power and even the bedroom of their wife whom they thought they had conquered. The less intelligent among them followed the Minister's example, getting caught up in promises and lies incapable of convincing anyone. And when they stumbled and fell, like a businessman threatened by financial ruin, like a politician forced into exile, like Don Juan having lost all his charm and discovering his teeth rotted out, his mind empty, and the agony of loneliness, they claimed that their lies had provoked their decline. The master was generous, but he had no pity for these renegades. The most intelligent among them turned their worries to their advantage. The Great Antoine's blessing could transform into anger and suddenly permit anyone to refuse them passage. Usually they wore an amulet, the sign of their power. A madras, a golden ring, a little metallic box containing a tooth and a lock of hair. The swindlers whose weapons were trickery and imitation, they disappeared for a week, having hidden themselves away at an accomplice's house, and then they emerged pretending to have returned from a visit to the master who had granted them protection. So, don't say you haven't been warned!

There were also folks that said Antoine of Gommiers never loaned his support to tricksters and wisely opposed ordinary weaknesses such as vanity and greed. He happily reminded his visitors that they all possessed the capacity for at least a little good. As mysterious as they may have appeared, his predictions were the result of an instinctive grasp of the causes and consequences that linked the past, present, and the future. What many thought of as a talent was really an art that doubled as friendship—the great desire to see the path you carry within.

The day when Antoinette collapsed in the street, her merchandise spilling out in every direction, the great Antoine had already seen everything, understood everything, foretold everything. Why didn't he rise from the grave in his white suit, causing woodpigeons and turtledoves to fly out of his hat like Antoinette dreamed about the night before! The one spoke so well, who mastered rhetorical devices without having to take classes with Maître Cantave, he could have said: Pick your head up. Look up, they're flying, the woodpigeons and turtledoves fluttering in your dreams. Look at that little one, up there all alone, settling in like an adult, setting himself apart from the group. Look at this couple of lovebirds held together like a promise. Look at the little one, he's coming back. The elders, his parents, they're happy. "Happy like Ulysses," Maître Cantave would've said. Franky could recite it by heart. You, too, can be happy, your sons will discover their wings. Let's go, stand up. Don't go. It's not over, this path you carry within. The birds in your dreams, they're real. Can't you hear them sing? Forge your own destiny, something other than this shit. Follow the path of the song, it will guide you far away. And everything that happened before will no longer matter.

The birds came for you. You called and they came with their songs. If only you could fly, you could touch them. But you were right to place your bet on their wings. As many wings as tickets. Moïse is the one who will be happy with all the money he'll owe you. And the people of the alleyway will applaud, even the jealous ones, shouting: "She won! The Doyenne won!" Are you aware of the saying "even as a bird walks, it's aware of its wings"? You hobbled all the way. But the wings don't fail the bird. All while you were hobbling, their wings flapped in silence. Please, don't die. The path you carry within, it's only just begun. Here comes the spreading of the wings. Place your bet on their wings. Here, here they are, the winning numbers in tomorrow's drawing. The jackpot, it'll be all yours. And the second. And the third. Fifty, fifteen, ten. For Antoinette, the one who dreamed of wings. So you can afford a life of your own. Don't go. Take your time. Damn it, don't die. You deserve to live before you die.

And three years later, if Antoine was as almighty as they say, that day when Franky got his head caught in the electrical wires and fell from the roof of the building he was helping us repaint, that day when Danilo and I picked him up, his body nearly broken in two, his kidneys ruptured on the edge of the sidewalk, his hair and his skull giving off a scent of burning flesh, why wasn't Antoine there to tell Franky: "Get away from there, don't climb so high, run along and write an essay, a poem, dream about the past, read from an old book; get out of here, you're going to fall. This work isn't meant for you—roofs, the smell of paint, cables frayed by clandestine electrical outlets. Get out of here and go pretend to be a poet or a chronicler, spare your legs the trouble." Danilo always came by with little side hustles. One Sunday, we had some buildings to paint. Someone with some money to throw away or to launder had bought and renovated them. Franky joined us. To earn some money. This was after the dispute with the history professor when he found himself unemployed. He didn't talk about it, but it bothered him that I was the only one bringing in any money. I didn't dare tell him no. We started at dawn. At night, you couldn't see a thing. You've got to paint the roof in the morning. By midday, to escape the sun, we would go paint the inside. The edging was all that was left. The ladder was too short. We had climbed onto the roof from the third story window. Danilo laughed, leaning into the open space to fill in those damn edges. He called me over. I came over to join him, and we laughed at the people walking by beneath us. Magdalène who, for once, had abandoned her preferred position. Mathias was ill, so she had to make a trip to the pharmacy. The director of the private institution Le Savoir doing his Sunday rounds, visiting female students under the pretext of private lessons. The mothers forcefully dragging their daughters to the temple that was the Église de la Dernière Chance. The little girls hobbled in their ill-fitting shoes; and the mothers spitefully glared at one another, suspicious, their eyes always on the look-out, if you so much as dare a glance, a pout, a gesture, or a comment suggesting your daughter is better dressed than mine... Miniatures, that's all we are. Miniatures perched high above, laughing at our miniature neighbors. Franky wanted to join us. To not be left out. To be part of the club. We never stopped criticizing him for always being alone and for not acting like everyone else. With other people. This time he acted normal. With other people. There was no Antoine of Gommiers or any other element of style. Just three wires from the corridor on the roof of a building on Grand Rue. Walking towards us, he caught his foot in the bucket of paint. While trying to collect himself he fell backward, and his head brushed against the cable. Only just brushed. Then it was as though the cable came to life and sucked him in from the back of his skull. Immediately, it smelled of burning flesh. Sparks. The horrible noise of bursts of lightning. Franky's body convulsing, dancing like a lunatic. And when the cable had taken from him all that it wished, his hair, the skin on his head, and a portion of his brain, it pushed him away with the same violence with which it had initially zapped him. His body was thrown forward, flying over our heads and landing among the miniature people below. Where was he on that day, the great Antoine? He predicted neither the fall, nor the doctors. Danilo and I came down. We could hear the voices of the people standing over Franky's body, screaming "he's dead!" We also thought he was dead. Even still, we drove him to the nearest hospital. The emergency room was closed. The doctors didn't come in on Sundays. The second hospital had doctors on staff, but not enough beds nor proper medical supplies. Finally, the third hospital had doctors, medical supplies, and open beds. One of the more suspicious doctors took a closer look at the body and shouted "no!" he wasn't dead. Almost dead. And so, they took him away, motionless and smelling of burnt flesh. A dislodged miniature. Almost dead. The top half nearly severed from the bottom. The smell of burnt flesh, it lingered for months. It took everything, time, operations, and treatments to clean him up, to remove the burnt flesh. This unbanked fire in his head. These bits of rotten flesh. Where was he, the great Antoine? And every night I spent looking after him, the people of the corridor awaited my return in the morning. There was just enough time for me to wash up before making my way to the bank. I felt the urge to wish good luck to people who placed bets according to the details of Franky's accident. There were many in the corridor. I heard them tell one another: "You must not wish ill upon your brother or your neighbors, they're family. Franky's a kind young man who's always got his mind elsewhere." They concluded: "Alas, life is what it is, just life." Soon the time would come when the saying "from bad comes good" became a reality for those banking their hopes and dreams on games of chance. So, what are the numbers for cable, fall, and paint?

In a country full of adversity where it is said 'dèyè mòn, gen mòn, beyond mountains there are mountains,' another particular feature of Gommiers is its vast plain that leads to the sea. It is a restless sea that does not necessarily spark the urge to take a dip. The so-called sons of the first and second secretaries of the master agreed, however, on one thing. Antoine of Gommiers was hardly a well-built man or an athlete. He would sometimes set out at dawn, and after a long walk punctuated by stops to greet the acacias and the eucalyptuses—his preferred trees, apart from the soursop trees—he would reach the coast, take off his clothing, and plunge into these waters, known for being too strong for the likes of man. This oracle of wisdom, whose knowledge foretold the dangers of obsession and excess, dared an act that only senseless children had attempted before. A few had given their lives to the sea, consumed by the currents, their bodies never to be recovered. The luckiest among them had been rescued by fishing boats. Taken back to their parents by the seafaring fishermen, the children fell into a delirium for months, swearing that beneath the sea they had witnessed a myriad of colors and encountered fantastical creatures that they could not even describe. Nightmares invaded their dreams, and after having tried every possible remedy, potions and prayers, their parents finally took them to see the master. He locked himself with the rescued child for a moment in the room of treasures as the son of the first secretary called it, or the workshop according to the son of the second secretary. The worried parents, gathered in the courtyard, overheard the laughter of children, voices full of youth, as though there were two kids having fun inside. Then the sick child emerged, perky and grinning, with the slightly less smiling master in tow. Antoine of Gommiers greeted the grateful family with a wave of his hat. Before the family's departure, the child and the seer exchanged one final glance, and it felt like their eyes shared a vigor and a complicity of old friends who had seen their way through many of life's challenges and pitfalls together. He confided in his secretaries the secret he shared with the children: it's not what you see that matters most, but what you make of what you see.

The parents of the children rescued from the point of Gommiers tried everything, from idle threats to gifts, exhausting the repertoire of ruses parents use to betray a child's vigilance. Not a single child revealed the content of the conversation they held with the master. And every one of them, those who left to make a life for themselves either in the capital or abroad, excelling in their professions to the point of notoriety, just like those content to live the life of a small-time farmer, never leaving their natal Grande Anse, returned to find the master at regular intervals, their hands overflowing with seashells.

Antoine of Gommiers knew how to be old with the elders, and youthful with the youngsters. One thing was for certain, nobody had ever seen such a swimmer in a region where there was nothing metaphoric about the expression "like a fish in water." The wild beaches of Gommiers were the most dangerous part of the coast, they only attracted lunatics. But for dozens of kilometers, the people of Grande Anse were people of the sea. Swimming was a part of everyday life, and all along the peninsular coastline, there were numerous swimmers whose prowess remained engraved in peoples' memories. Everyone remembered the poet who claimed to be a sea bass. Abandoning the composition of an ode to the sea, he dove from his tiny pleasure boat to save a military officer who was sent to quell yet another imaginary uprising from the currents. The powers-that-be felt that the region was too quiet. Some threat must have been brewing. Repression was the best weapon of prevention. A brutal, high-ranking officer was needed to conduct such a mission. The members of the death squad had witnessed their leader, a scoundrel and author of many bloodthirsty crimes under the influence of a higher power, turn his back on the mission and wade into the sea with a robotic cadence. Soon, he became nothing more than a little dot, barely larger than the boat of the seafaring poet. Many opinions changed hands: did he do the right thing by saving this man, a rapist and torturer? Was this person's life worth suspending the composition of a poem and risking his own life in exchange? But everyone recognized that the seafaring poet, while he was not necessarily a master wordsmith or navigator, was one hell of a swimmer. He spent two whole hours dragging a body weighed down by crimes and heavy metal to the shore.

The rescued man then resigned from the army, begged for his victims' forgiveness, avoided the sea, and visited every holy site he could in search of repentance. The seafaring poet sold his boat and gave up his pursuit of the muse's call, contenting himself with giving swimming lessons.

The folks of Grand Anse also remembered the Mombin brothers, whose skiff was battered and overturned by a hurricane. The Mombin twins did everything together. They got married on the same day to two of the most beautiful women in the region, women who were coveted by the young men of the bourgeoisie and the local representatives of the public administration. The women refused everyone's proposals to wed the Mombin brothers. The twins boasted nothing more than a dilapidated house, a small-time fishing business, and a reputation as fighters. The two couples lived in the same house, they ate lunch together beneath the veranda, and they accompanied one another to the evening ball at the local harvest festival, where the wives danced in a manner the jealous locals judged too lascivious for one's husband as well as for one's brother-in-law. Rumor has it that the four secretly took turns with one another in their decrepit abode.

The Mombin twins were setting out to catch sea turtles. Despite the portending signs of an oncoming hurricane, nobody thought to discourage them. The Mombin brothers always did as they pleased anyway. And their eventual disappearance did not exactly bother the chivalrous locals already primed to go on the prowl for their widows. The furious winds lasted an entire day. When the calm was restored, all there was left to account for was the devastation, the destroyed plantations, the trees torn from their roots, the roofs blown off, and to count the dead and those who had disappeared. The Mombin brothers were the first to be listed among the disappeared. Their wives were beautiful, and full of youth. The prefect, the mayor, the district commander, the local bureaucrats, and the important clerks rushed to the widows' house, their eyes overflowing with a desire hardly commensurate with a visit to express their condolences. The awkward coterie even went so far as to advise the women to allow themselves a brief period of mourning followed by a rapid return, accompanied by the mundane joys of life. Three days after the passage of the hurricane, the Mombin brothers emerged from the water, exhausted, and covered in scrapes and bruises, their skin burned by the sun, the two of them carrying an enormous sea turtle. They walked peacefully towards their house where their wives welcomed them home like heroes. The night of their return, the two couples invited the local elite and the victims of the storm to join them and share in a turtle stew.

Grande Anse had no shortage of great swimmers. But the peasants claiming to be the sons of the first and second secretaries of the master were blunt. Their fathers, men who never told a lie, admitted they had never seen a better, more gorgeous swimmer than Antoine of Gommiers. He moved through the water with complete and utter grace, calming the waves with his strokes, escorted by the flight of blue herons and kingfishers. As soon as he turned around, the birds, which fled the commerce of mankind by instinct, stood on the beach to wait for him. After putting his clothing back on and regaining the appearance of an ordinary man, he started on his return home, walking at a gentle pace, so softly that he did not disturb the agoutis and the mabouya. The peasants he *encountered along the way greeted him, saying "Bonjou, master." He replied using his right index finger to tip his hat, and sometimes he stopped long enough to have a coffee or a tea in the tiny house of a peasant family to bring them the news, but only if the news was good.*

The sea. A load of shit. I recalled the lyrics from one of the singers Franky invited to the viewing, foaming at the mouth like a rabid dog. *"Lanmè Pòtoprens yon lanmè fatra anba pye. M ta fout li on kout tanbou raboday nan bounda l, pou ofinal li pote non lanmè. The sea of Port-au-Prince, a sea of trash beneath your feet. I'd give it a swift kick of the raboday drum in the ass, so that when it's all said and done, she bears the name of the sea."* I could've told him, the singer, given him some real information he could use to improve his couplet. I could've told him that even if you're already angry with the sea, there's no use in kicking it. Beneath the surface, there's something solid that scrapes the skin and fractures the bone. Franky and me, we tried it out when we were fourteen years old. We were a little embarrassed we'd never set foot in this place that everyone talked about. Drugs. Clandestine departures. The drowned. The haunted looks on the faces of survivors forcefully repatriated by the American Coast Guard. Day trips organized by neighborhood. Even the Église de la

Dernière Chance organized an outing every year, supervised by the deacons and the pastor. Bikinis were prohibited, and compulsory prayers before swimming. Forbidden also were those couples and their escapades on private beaches along the road to the south. The girls always returned full of melancholy. And the boys, their heads held high like a cock's, declared that in the sea you could have sex without protection because salt was even better than citrus at protecting against viruses and microbes. The sea was something you had to get to know. The fact that we had never waded into its waters was one of our greatest flaws. Antoinette never had the money for the planned day trips. Or, if she did have it, she hated to imagine us so far away from her. Walking was her way of life. Her trademark. Not ours. To her, the only place we were allowed to go without running any risk was nowhere at all. This is also probably why she preferred Franky. Apart from running off to his conference presentations and this madness of going to Gommiers, Franky preferred to take walks in his head. For that matter, he didn't exactly give the impression that he was suffering as he remained glued to his seat. He had the old books that Savior brought him, his pencils, his notebooks, Antoine's life story that he worked on every day from morning to night. I noticed him laughing as he writes and, without telling him, I'm glad to know that writing brings him a little bit of joy. As for his chair, I'm not so sure. Even if he doesn't let anything on, along with his asthma, it must torture him to suffer from these legs that no longer have any use, having to ask for help to move from one place to another. The silence between us has become its own activity, one of those everyday acts to which we devote our energy to complete the façade. These are tricks you use to better portray a character, a version of us fit for others. To avoid boring everyone, sometimes you provide a summary, a few details, an appearance. And everyone's delighted to be able to say to themselves, "Look, there's what's-his-name!" before moving on to something else.

We wanted to get to know the sea. We knew that the waters by Port-au-Prince weren't exactly the ideal place to make its acquaintance. But even the ocean divides us. When you don't have a boat to reach open water or a sandy path leading to a beach worthy of such a name, you make do with what you have. You're happy with what's accessible. Exiting of the alley, an accessible beach isn't far. It smells like gasoline, and to the right, you see the wharf and the big commercial ships. To the left, there's nothing to see. It's the same watery expanse, if you can even call it water, extending into infinity. About thirty minutes. All you do is exit the alley onto Grand Rue. Enter the Cité. The Cité, where the real bosses, the real gangs, the real poor people live. There, where you walk without lifting your gaze or looking at the people you pass along the way. I don't know how they manage to recognize that you're an outsider. That you live somewhere else. Even when that somewhere else is so close by. Even when you have nothing, just like them. The people from the Cité a believe, even if you have nothing, if you're from somewhere else, it can't possibly be the same as their nothing. They stick together and don't tolerate stares. At the end of the Cité there's the sea.

There were lots of people there. Boys our age. And

one real little kid. Seven or eight years old, tops. With lumpy inner tubes to float on. The first disappointment: we were looking for somewhere else, this was nothing more than an extension of the Cité. We saw more plastic bottles than water. And the water, it was neither blue nor green. I don't even think it was water anymore, but a thick sauce that takes on the dark colors of the ingredients it's made of. The sea of Port-au-Prince, it's a mixture of water and whatever we throw into it. The second disappointment, especially for Franky, who by virtue of his belief in fairy tales, got it into his head that once you're in the sea all men become brothers. The group of boys didn't consider us brothers at all and shot us overtly threatening looks. Only the little one seemed to have taken sympathy upon us and came closer toward us. The only one who said hello to us. The others scanned us from top to bottom like we didn't belong and shouted that he shouldn't sympathize with foreigners. It was the first time we'd been treated like foreigners. Up to that point, foreigners had always meant someone else. A lost *Blan*, looking for an "artist" who lived in the alley. A young man, dressed too well, sent by a real estate company to inspect an abandoned building or a set of buildings "for sale" along Grand Rue. The drivers of luxury cars whizzing by with apologies and fear in their eyes as we exchanged looks.

"Well, they're boys just like us." And the little boy continued to move toward us, smiling and holding out his hand. If you don't have any power, nobody likes to be a foreigner. Foreign can mean two things. Uninvolved, just passing through, and powerful. Or particularly vulnerable and ignorant of the laws of the land. We were in the second category.

It was heartening to see the little boy oppose the older boys' chess match and treat us like fellow human beings. Small and brave. He offered to loan us his inner tube for a few minutes. "You'll see, once you ignore the trash, it's kind of nice. You sit in the middle of the inner tube, and then you let someone move you around." It was our first time. We didn't know how it worked. "I'll help you." We took off our shirts and stepped into the sea made of more than just water. I had hidden our cash in a plastic bag in the pocket of my shorts. We never had enough money to be taking any risks. We kept our shoes on. Together with the little boy, we walked over metal plates, plastic bottles, scrap metal, chunks of concrete. Everything humans could have made use of floated beneath our feet. Then the little boy sat Franky on top of the inner tube and joked: "You look like a king" The king's butt was in the water. Me, I had my legs. "Just like me. You'll serve the king." The little boy had spirit. Okay, serve the king. I joined him. One hand on the inner tube. Kicking his feet, he pushed us. The further we moved forward—the water up to our waists, our faces—the more I felt that something lying dormant was about to come alive. If he had asked me, I would have told the singer with the enraged voice that he was mistaken. The trash wasn't under our feet. But all around us. And bits of I don't even know what floated to the surface and smacked us right in the face. The boy continued to push us. Into the open water. I was already on the tips of my toes, he kept pushing. Then he said: "Alright, I'll leave you to it." He made his way to the shore, swimming like a fish, and joined his friends. With his asthma and all the trash floating around the two of us, Franky started to panic. He flailed his hands in every direction and the dirty water he flung around splashed me in the face and got in my mouth. One hand clinging to the inner tube, I searched for the bottom. Something to push against to pull us forward. Seek, and you shall find. Something more powerful than the sole of my shoes punctured the sole of my foot. That's right, comrade singer, the sea of Port-au-Prince, a sea of metal beneath your feet. Franky was out of breath. I was bleeding. I didn't notice the blood until later. In the list of ingredients that make up the sea of Port-au-Prince, there are also drops of blood. Being afraid is a feeling that Franky and I have often shared. A fear of the dark. A fear of being caught by Antoinette after we'd done something stupid. A fear of the devil. When we were little and we heard the noise of birds landing on the roof, we thought it was the devil himself coming to get us. The fear of catching a disease in Doriane's tiny bedroom, our first prostitute and our first lover. A fear of stray bullets when, for some reason or another, the night took Grand Rue by surprise. A fear of Baba, one of Pépé's associates who threatened to beat the shit out of us because Joanna, his girlfriend, his property, was taking secretarial classes and sometimes came by to have Franky help her with her homework. At fourteen years old, when you live on one of the streets leading to Grand Rue, you think you're a bigshot, precocious, and in your own mind you've already seen all there is to fear. But all our past fears, they were nothing more than hypotheticals. Not death in real time. The sea of Port-au-Prince penetrated our lungs while we sank deeper, drifting into open water. We were going to die. We didn't dare look at one another. Antoine of Gommiers, couldn't have seen this coming. We couldn't die and leave Antoinette all alone. Who would accompany her to the bank to buy her lottery tickets? Who would she tell her farfetched stories? And who would she beat on after daring to express doubt? And, what would she tell herself afterwards? That I dragged Franky into this? For Antoinette, one always drags the other into something bad. Danilo drags me into it, and I drag Franky. Danilo told me not to wander into that rotten sea. Wait. He was working on a plan so that, one day, the three of us could go to a real sea. Some ideas occur to Franky and me simultaneously, without any need for discussion. And when it happens, nothing can hold us back. And so, we were going to drown together. In this filthy sea. What's that element of style in Franky's repertoire called? The one where you accept both meanings of the word, the literal and the figurative. A filthy sea in every sense of the word. We didn't think about the meaning. When death is certain, what's the point in thinking about it! Resurrection being improbable. I heard the boy's voice calling out to us, waving at us with his hands. His ten fingers spread wide, then his fists closed. Four times in a row. And another gesture with his hand, creasing imaginary bills. I understood. Forty *goud*. OK. Forty *goud* in service of the king and his servant. Humor wasn't all this kid had. He swam towards us. For a few interminable seconds, we wondered if he would get here in time. He did. Perfect timing. He must have calculated the whole thing. He helped Franky sit back on the inner tube correctly. The king's ass was back in the water, and I clung with both hands to the side of the inner tube. The kid told us to calm down, to quit making useless and chaotic movements and to just let him lead us back. His voice no longer had the softness of a suggestion.

The voice of a leader. We obeyed his commands like docile sheep. He took us back ashore, and while we put our shirts back on, he told me the time had come to pay up before his friends got angry. I took the plastic bag out of my shorts, and the money out of the bag. Without rancor. In a world where survival depends on your ability to cope, forty *goud* is a cheap price to pay for allowing yourself to forget that the appearance of kindness is a slippery slope leading right into a trap. We simply forgot. Forty *goud* for our naïveté. In my little plastic bag, there was only thirty-seven *goud*. The little boy's friends formed a circle around us and wanted to beat the crap out of us over the three missing *goud*. "It's alright," he said, "we'll let them go." My foot was still bleeding. He gave me back five goud. "To buy some tetracycline. I don't know what you cut yourself on: some iron, a nail, an old bone. Anyway, you'll need a few doses otherwise your whole body could start to rot." I told him thanks. "Let's go home, guys." The others obeyed him, mumbling, and broke apart the circle. A true little leader. And clever to boot. With just a little bit of kindness to spare for the antibiotics, nobody forced him to do that. As for the sea, that was our first time, and our last. Still, to this day, I have no idea what I cut myself on. I like to think that it was a piece of iron instead of a bone. There you go, my songwriter, add that to your inventory. Bones also lie in the sea of Port-au-Prince. And I don't know what scared me more. The fear of abandoning Antoinette. The disapproving words she would have pronounced to my dead body for having dragged her beloved Franky to his death. The feeling that I was going to die. Or the idea of losing my brother. I never saw the little boy again. I tell myself that, in service of some sort of cause, whether good or evil, with the face of an angel and the genius of a trickster, he would make one hell of a leader.

Besides the services to the gods, *which only the tiny community of the lakou attended, the only collective gatherings led by Antoine of Gommiers consisted of the monthly blessings. On the third Tuesday of every month, before sunrise, his secretaries installed a few rows of benches in the lakou, along with a grand table on which goblets and carafes of water were placed, the master's rocking chair in front of the benches, and a little table and two chairs sat in front of the rocker. At eight o'clock, the first secretary opened the wooden gate situated in the center of the fence made of candelabra and other cactuses and let the crowd in. The second secretary ensured that nobody cheated, so the first to arrive went to be seated in the front row. Order was respected and the second secretary's surveillance was a gesture that was more symbolic than necessary. When the benches were nearly full and there was only one row left, the second secretary dispatched a child to tell the first secretary to close the gate. The protestations and pleas from those left on the outside fell on deaf ears. Desperate, those seeking a* *blessing stood a while longer outside the hedgerow of cactuses, attempting to see between two branches what was unfolding in the lakou. At eight thirty, the master left his house, robed in white, holding a little bell in his hand. The two secretaries went to stand behind him, the first to his right, the second to his left. The gathering could begin. The master rang his little bell. The first blessing-seeker rose to his feet, walked toward the grand table, and poured himself a glass of water. No one could come near the master without submitting to this purifying ritual. Then, with a sign from the first secretary, the blessing-seeker approached the little table, and, while standing, placed on it the object for which he sought a blessing. With a sign from the second secretary, he sat down in one of the chairs, awaiting the master's verdict. His blessing was denied. Without addressing them directly or according to them the leisure of a seat, the master dismissed with a flick of his left hand the men and women who had placed on the table a weapon, a pair of underwear, bank notes or coins—obvious symbols of a desire for power and dominion. Depending on how their request was received, the visitors left with a hop in their step, or their backs hunched. Watching them pass through the gate held open for them by the child left standing guard, the disappointed crowd gathered outside guessed at the fate of each demand. Everything gave rise to competition; they had managed to turn it into a game. With the arrival of each blessing-seeker, the winner was the first to shout: "Denied" or "Accepted."*

The so-called sons of the first and second secretaries recorded two exceptional instances during these monthly blessings. One normal Tuesday, while the benches were already full of blessing-seekers, Antoine of Gommiers took a seat in his rocker and, contrary to the custom, he did not ring his little bell, and ordered the second secretary to go find in the crowd of people left outside a boy with hair the color of cinnamon wearing a blue hat and shoes that were too big for his feet. The first secretary went out and immediately recognized the boy, a scrawny kid with a blank stare. In the meantime, upon the master's orders, the first secretary had brought a pinch of indigo from the workshop. The first secretary guided the stupefied boy toward the large table and poured a goblet of water for him. To the surprise of both secretaries, the master signaled for the child to approach him with the goblet in hand, without requiring him to drink from it. Antoine of Gommiers invited the boy to take a seat in one of the two chairs. The boy sat down and took from his pocket a folded sheet of paper that he unfolded to place on the table. The two secretaries, daring not to lean their heads over the master's shoulders, made out the lines of a clumsy drawing that could have represented an overturned thatched roof, a hat with sharp, pointy edges, or a rowboat. Antoine of Gommiers spread across the four corners of the sheet the pinch of powder from the plant, which, according to the wise, corresponds to the seventh color of the rainbow, and motioned to the boy to wash it away with the water. The master then took the page stained with marks of blue, shook it in midair, and blew on it to chase away the drops of water before returning it to the boy. The boy left, walking awkwardly in his oversized dress shoes, but with a less stupefied gaze than before.

Three weeks later, the proprietor and editor-in-chief of the periodical "Ad Libitum", who, still obese and suffering back pain, had hardly recovered from the conditions of his back-

*and-forth trips between Jérémie and Port-au-Prince, dedicat-
ed an entire issue to story that sent shockwaves through the
capital: the unexpected escape of a convicted felon. The man,
a domestic and handyman for a residence in Pétion-Ville, had
been accused of murdering the family who employed him: the
father, mother, and their three children. They had all been
hacked to pieces with a machete. The house, a gingerbread with
decorative woodwork that fascinated architectural enthusiasts
and persnickety artists alike, had retained its external beauty.
The bodies, however, had been chopped to bits and the walls of
the bedrooms, the family room, and the kitchen were covered
in blood as though the assassin wished to paint everything red,
apart from the little sitting room, where there were cigarette
butts in an ashtray, an empty teapot and cup, still lukewarm,
proof that the murderer had sat there after having committed
the crime. According to the maid's account, a pair of the master's shoes were missing and a few pieces of the mistress's jewelry. The gardener-deliveryman-porter-watchman disregard-
ed the jewelry's disappearance. As for the shoes, his employer
found them out of style, worn out, and so he offered them to
him. Having few occasions to wear dress shoes, he gave them
to his son who, perhaps, would not end up a domestic laborer like himself. His mother was out of the picture for a long
time, so the son lived alone. The man's employers had refused
to allow the boy to share the carriage house in which he slept.
He didn't have the means to offer his son gifts often, nor did
he see as much of him as he would have liked. The day of the
crime, taking advantage of his weekly day off, he took his son
for a walk in the city. The boy was a little slow and suffered
from a speech impediment. Despite the absence of additional*

*proof, the domestic laborer was charged. The rumor circulat-
ed that the head of the family, a coffee exporter as well as an
importer of luxury products, was on the brink of bankruptcy,
crippled with debt and threatened by his angry creditors. Folks
had also said that the mother had declined the advances of a
military general incapable of hearing "no" for an answer and
capable of the worst excesses. In the most tightly knit circles,
folks even claimed that the family, the adults and the children
alike, regularly held costumed orgies modeled on the Roman
bacchanalia. The domestic, a native of Grand Anse, possessed
only this son for family. The child himself, an adolescent who
everyone declared retarded, lived alone in a tiny house his
father rented for the year and, because the boy had never
developed the art of conversation, spent his time drawing.
Even the boy's solitude and his passion for drawing played
out against the father. According to the accusation, what kind
of moral character can be attributed to a man who abandons
his own child, leaving his son to fend for himself? In one of
the boy's sketchbooks, they found a drawing representing five
hanging figures, two adults and three children. Since the truth
emerges from the hands and mouths of children, the magis-
trates concluded that the father had confessed to his son. The
defense hardly had the chance to argue that five hanging figures
in a drawing did not necessarily have anything to do with five
bodies mutilated with a machete before the man was tried and
convicted to a life of forced labor. The only leave he was granted was a weekly visit from his son, who brought him drawings
that he used to paper the walls of his cell. The public opinion
remained divided. The conservatives, believing in the foul nature of poor people and the proximity between domestics and*

their employers too powerful a temptation for the first and a dangerous promiscuity for the second, supported the verdict, lamenting that the bandit had escaped the death penalty. The radicals with a penchant for dissent, folks who always found ways to poke holes in arguments and blamed society for all of the ills from which it suffered, saw in the condemnation of the domestic an easy way to avoid a real investigation, the results of which would have doubtlessly incriminated the wealthy by revealing the fraudulent nature of their financial transactions, their sleazy habits, and their adherences to Thanatos' cult.

The editor-in-chief, director-proprietor of the periodical "Ad Libitum" had written in his gazette: "A moment not for the faint of heart: the convicted criminal Alésius Fontin, prisoner for life, has literally disappeared from his cell in the national penitentiary. He had received a visit from his son in the afternoon. The adolescent had been searched upon his arrival and had nothing more in his possession than a few drawings. Correctional officers at the penitentiary confirmed that after his visit that they had closed the door to his cell. The detainee seemed calm and pleasant. On the final search of the day, he was lying on his mattress and everything led the guards to believe that he was sleeping. The next morning, the cell was empty. After questioning the personnel, the complicity of one or several guards was ruled out. A complete mystery. How, like in a riddle of a locked room, could he have escaped from his cell? This got people talking. Folks put forth hare-brained hypotheses. The winner goes to those whispering about shadows walking along the rooftops of the penitentiary or the ghost-ships, proof positive that at the conclusion of the ordeal at number 22 Route Nationale, minds are just as superstitious in the capital as in our provinces."

The two secretaries were not readers of the periodical "Ad Libitum" whose print run did not exceed more than fifty or so mimeographed copies. The echoes, however, reverberated all the way to Gommiers. They hurried to the master and found him drowsing in his rocker. Upon their arrival, he opened his eyes and said: "The pathway out is often the same as the one leading in." He closed his eyes once more and fell back into a slumber without leaving them the chance to say a single word.

What a joke. This story about the blues must be what got Franky hooked. Still, he's more qualified than most to understand that humans can't fly. We never talk about his accident. It's something that happened. We just had to live with the consequences. Whenever some curious stranger starts looking for the details, we divert the conversation. Well, lucky for us, we encounter very few strangers. The alley isn't a place that people tend to visit to forge new friendships. Here, we have lifelong friendships with people who share our condition. If someone made the mistake of telling us they come to us as a friend, we'd know right away that they lead a life worse than ours and that they're looking for the words to start over. You'd have to really be up shit's creek to find the land of your dreams in the alley. There are already too many of us. Danilo sometimes has a funny way of looking at it. When the screaming from one household invades the alley and a little girl goes walking through the neighborhood begging for a place to stay, he says you shouldn't be sad.

"Someone had the brilliant idea of freeing up some empty space." All Franky and I have is a two-room house. More like one room cut in two by a burlap curtain. Before, it used to be one half for Antoinette and the other half for us. There's only one light on the ceiling, and Franky loves to read at night. He tolerated the need for lights out. The light impeded Antoinette's dreams. She needed the darkness for her body to relax and for her dreams to come alive. Now that she's no longer here, Franky has the half with the window, and I have the door. In the alley, everyone's room is more or less identical. But sometimes there's an army of children piled in on top of one another, while on the other side there's a woman poorer than Antoinette who continues to churn them out with men who come for sex and then disappear. That's a father for you. Like us, Danilo never knew his father. He says that if every father got it in their heads to live with their children, the population of the alleys would nearly double. It would be a never-ending war between aging machos and a real bummer for the women who already have a hard enough time dealing with their children. Danilo puts it like this: "Believe me, kolonn, whether a dead or absent father, you've got to appreciate his kindness for giving everyone else a little bit of space." Franky doesn't like this joke because it shows a lack of respect for the dead. Franky, the dead, and respect. Tradition. Origins. These notebooks he fills with notes. There are times when I wonder if he believes in it. If it's like some kind of prank he wants to play on whoever would waste their time reading these tales of the master, secretaries, and miracle seekers. Often, from the other side of the curtain, I catch him laughing and slapping his paralyzed legs. Laughing like a kid having fun. And then, there are these long writing sessions where he doesn't laugh at all. I'll see him focused, recopying, consulting old books, and crossing out lines. Then he'll push his chair backwards, causing him to fall into bed and drift into sleep exhausted. During the night, I swipe his already full notebook. The next morning, I return it to its place. I have a hard time with his lengthy sentences. That must be it, his style. Some sentences linger on for a while, dancing on a wire without ever losing their balance. And his vocabulary! So many refined words, just like in books. I feel like my head is spinning. "Good God!" As Moïse would shout when a fake news story comes out, something like "the government has acted on the behalf of the people, the senate voted in favor of a law granting farmers access to loans." Moïse, he listens to Métro-Machin, but I think it's just so that he can make himself angry. "Good God! Get out of here, you bastards!" I wonder if he's not secretly a little bit of a communist or something like that. He holds meetings in his house in Bas Peu de Chose with dudes who look like the singer at Antoinette's wake. All he needed was a little blue... When one of the guys in his crew was picked up by the police, with all the money that Pépé paid the judge to get him out of prison, he could've bought tons of indigo. Maybe I'm the one who's getting my leg pulled. Franky has got to know that I'm reading his notes, that I don't get everything. And, besides that, I don't believe a single word. So, he piles it on. Just to piss me off. To piss me off, maybe that's too strong. Maybe, just to get on my nerves. When we were kids, he was the teaser. I pretended to get angry. Antoinette would think we were fighting, and pull the ancestor card, her Antoine of

Gommiers, to remind us that fighting between brothers is always a grave mistake. She also reminded us of the sort of tragedies that befell those who continue in the error of their ways. "If you continue in the error of your ways..." Thanks, Mr. Wise Guy. We didn't need her or her Antoine to understand. Antoinette always thought we were more precious and naive than we were. Maybe it's just the way mothers are. Giving themselves reasons to sacrifice their own lives to play the guardian angel. After our guardian angel died, Franky wanted to get a job. The director of the institution Le Savoir hired him as a teacher. The pay was terrible. And always behind. Franky hated playing the disciplinarian. He came home at night cursing the director who only cared about the money and who ordered the teachers to take it easy when grading the work of their paying students. The one he really hated was the history teacher. A moron. The students dozed off while he taught his class. I pointed out "Kolonn, not everyone is like you. Most people don't enjoy rifling through the past!" But he ignored my arguments, only getting more worked up. "He's wrong about everything, dates, the historical motives. I'm telling you, he's a real moron. He wound up scrapping with the moron. It's the first time in his life that he'd gotten into a fight. The director dismissed him. The students were finding it increasingly difficult to pay. And the moron had a diploma. Meanwhile, Franky earned his last paycheck. He used half of the money to pay for his pencils and notebooks. And old books. He piles it all into a trunk. His books, I've never touched them. The stories other people tell, I'm not interested. But reading the words Franky writes, it's a way for us to stay in touch. The two of us aren't really talkative. So, he writes, and I read. It's like a conversation. Even if the things he talks about feel like they're out of this world.

The second extraordinary occurrence linked to the blessing ceremonies the so-called sons of the first and second secretaries of Antoine of Gommiers reported is a story of love and death, or of death and love—the two narrators never agreeing on which of the two elements took precedence, "the death that awaits us and the love we call on," as the poet Leo Ferré once put it, that is, if you want to draw meaning or a particular moral from the story.

A couple that came in a private car was seated in the middle row. They were wealthy. The man, well put together, strong, in his forties, built like an athlete, looking very sure of himself. He must have been a winner, a man of character who knew how to get people to do his bidding. He gazed at dozens of blessing-seekers bowing their heads; some went so far as to rise from their seats, under the pretext of stretching their legs, to fully devote themselves to the pleasure of contemplation. The man's wife was a woman whose beauty far exceeded that of Jeanne, who served the master's coffee in the afternoons, she *was like the Hollywood stars who came to Antoine's ounfò in search of the secrets of eternal youth. According to the so-called son of the first secretary, the movie stars had left the master autographed pictures, some were naked and coquettish, others were dressed in evening gowns. According to the socalled son of the second secretary, there were no such pictures. In fact, the ladies disrobed long enough for a bath of leaves, accompanied by the ounsi's song in the workshop. The debate between the two was pointless and the details insignificant, especially since unanimity was reached on the most important thing. Never, in the secretaries' memory, more than one and a half decades of good and loyal service to their master, Antoine of Gommiers, the illustrious oungan and seer who received female visitors from all walks of life and every race, had they seen a comparable beauty enter the lakou, or any other locale. The first secretary had traveled to many of the islands of the Caribbean, working as a laborer in the fields by day, a server in a bar in the evening time, and, by night, he passed as a seer from Ginen. He had seen many women in his travels, and in service of his three functions. Outside his natal Grand Anse, the second secretary only knew the capital, where he had worked as a gardener for powerful families who hosted sumptuous receptions and received many foreign guests. Still, despite the difference between a city and an archipelago in size, the central point was established. Neither of the two, in their past lives up to the point when they began serving the master, nor after the master's death, when they were forced to abandon the lakou to establish a new way of life, had they seen a comparable beauty. The two so-called sons of the first and second secretaries had never seen the woman other than through the eyes of their fathers and so they could* not paint her portrait. The so-called son of the first secretary acknowledged that, if his father had indeed traveled the islands and made a few female conquests before entering the master's service, he was not a handsome man. But when he would talk about this woman, his coarse features suddenly became full of light. To avoid being outdone and to escape, at least once, his role of the son of the second, the so-called son of the second secretary presented his father as a very handsome man, constantly solicited by the maids and a few madams of the grand homes where he looked after the roses and orchids. However, a difficult childhood had endowed him with an extremely surly nature. He was a man of great fury. After the master's death, he started a family. To calm him down, his children invented a trick: all they had to do was ask him about this woman who came with her husband to participate in that one blessing ceremony. Then, his eyes plunged deep into a look of astonishment in no way impacted by the passage of time, he always began with a tender voice: "Oh, how beautiful she was!" Losing himself in a description more evocative than sacred love poems, he forgot about those gathered to listen and spoke directly to the absent woman, "Oh, how beautiful you are!" These expressions of admiration constituted his sole failure to fulfill his duties as a faithful husband and a responsible father.

Upon the couple's arrival, the wife wore a light scarf that veiled her face. Only, not until they had settled into their seats on the bench, did she lift it and hold it in her lap, liberating the beauty of her features, provoking a near riotous excitement in the gathered crowd of blessing-seekers. Antoine of Gommiers, robed in white with his tiny bell in hand, stepped out of his house, settled into his rocking chair, closed his eyes long enough *for everyone to take their seats again and settle down, opened his eyes once the silence was restored, and gestured to the couple to step toward him. Without offering them the leisure of sitting down, he addressed the husband first: "Return immediately to the hotel from whence you came and gaze upon your wife." He then turned to the wife, held out his left hand, into which she placed her silk scarf and whispered to her words that the two secretaries standing behind him could not make out clearly. Later in the day, they spent a little bit of time working to reconstruct the tenor of the words and concluded the master had said: "Never again." He then called forth one of the many nieces or little cousins in the lakou, a girl who answers to the name of Hortense or Hortensia, and who was the most skilled at climbing trees, and told her to tie the scarf to the highest branch of the tallest acacia. The couple left. The master rang his tiny bell to announce the beginning of the ordinary service. At the end of the service, the two secretaries, disappointed by the couple's dismissal—the woman was of such beauty that they would have hoped to never see her part—dared to ask the master why he had sent them away. He replied that the man, who appeared to them to be in good health and wished to covet the woman's beauty for himself alone by way of this veil, was going to die that night from an illness whose harmful effects were accelerated by the torments of jealousy. Death's victory over arrogance and conceit often comes by surprise. Without warning the man that his end was soon to come, Antoine advised him to enjoy his final moments by devoting himself to the activity from which he derived the most pleasure, even if, in his particular case, pleasure was linked to vanity. —And as for the scarf? In reality, the knot tied by the little girl was not tight enough and the wind had already lifted it far away. Maybe the scarf had flown, from branch to branch, out to sea. "Why worry about the scarf?" Nobody, nothing, must exist for the purpose of disguising beauty.*

The following year, on the anniversary of the couple's arrival at the blessing ceremony, at nightfall the master had set up a little table, two chairs, a storm lantern for a little light, a little bowl of breadfruit, a carafe of fresh water, a teapot containing an infusion of verbena and basil, and two enamel goblets at the verge of the lakou where the coastal plain could be seen in its vastness, all the way to the sea. Then an employee from the Jérémie Post Office arrived, begging pardon for showing up at such an hour. But he came to deliver a certified letter and that the person sending the letter—or rather, the woman sending it—had included the delivery fees all the way to Gommiers. The Post Office employee's vehicle had broken down, and he had to complete a decent part of the trip on foot. The master offered him a chair to sit on, some water to refresh himself, and some tea to warm his spirits. After a break, perked up by the warmth of the tea and the freshness of the water, the mailman placed his hat back on and left. The secretaries were worried to see him leave at night, but Antoine reassured them. The mailman would have a very good night. He had family at the base of the coastal plain, a female cousin who would welcome him with open arms.

There are no women in our lives now. Doriane was the first. We were still children. She was a child, too. But she already had a bedroom of her own, a business that was going well, and a reputation. Danilo always has a leg up on us in real life, he told us the price, showed us the way and how to approach her. Doriane chose her own clients. She didn't accept conquistadors or mopes. Before, she had a mother and a stepfather. Wear and tear had killed her mother. She had nothing against her stepfather. After the funeral, he simply wanted her to replace her mother. He pleaded with her in sadness. Begged her. Implored her. Promised her gifts he couldn't afford. It's thanks to the bigger bed that she accepted. While her mother was alive, she'd slept on a broken bed, too small to support her thirteen years. Her stepfather said: "I love you so much that I'll give you the large bed." It's thanks to the king bed that she accepted. And because he had always been good to her and her mother. Never vi-Olent or lazy. Mutually beneficial. The first night, he kept his promise and went to sleep, pleasant and docile, in the busted little bed. The second evening, he wanted to share the king-sized bed. And in the morning, he started making demands, laying out his expectations for meals, the state of the house, his unwashed shirts. Things that had nothing to do with the deal they'd made. When he returned in the evening, Doriane told him that she had come to a resolution that day. It included an offer and a demand. Here's the offer. The first few times, she let him have sex with her, not begrudgingly, but she was passive, a little indifferent. Tonight, she would make love to him. Not just in the evening. All night long, if he wished. And so, all night long, with cunning and cheer, she took him to new heights in the king-sized bed. In the morning, after a long kiss, she explained her demand: "Don't come back tonight. Don't ever come back." He never came back. And since then, she chooses the men who spend time in her king-sized bed. There have been men from the gang that Pépé had taken over, as well as police officers. Proving that she had protection on both sides. They're her only concession. She has criteria for accepting her real clients: don't behave like sex is rightfully yours, and don't behave like a wet blanket. Franky and I never had the means to think that anything was ever rightfully ours. We didn't behave like wet blankets either. We were just simply awkward and curious kids. We were the first clients who were the same age as her. She laughed and asked who was up first. I let Franky go and sat outside on the doorstep to wait. I didn't wait long. Then, Franky took my place on the doorstep. Pulling me toward the bed, she said that it was like making love to the same client twice. Afterwards, she concluded that we weren't identical, we didn't have the same bodies. We were the same without being identical. We had a few differences. The problem was this, every time we tried to express our differences, we wound up doing the same exact thing. At Doriane's, we wanted to go back alone, hiding it from one another. But as it happens, like a pair of idiots, we had chosen the same evening. She suggested we spare the wait outside. We accepted. On the way back home, we were happy. Despite the sound of bullets in the night and the grilling Antoinette would unleash upon our return.

Antoine of Gommiers

FIRST APPENDIX

Dear Antoine of Gommiers,

I'm writing to you from a foreign country that, as you predict-ed, is preparing itself for a war more deadly than all the rest. The imminence of war has created such a panic that people are going into hiding and are becoming suspicious of their neigh-bors. Others are spending money like their lives were coming to an end. The casinos, hotels that charge by the hour, movie theaters, and nightclubs never empty out.

I mentioned these four locations because I've found my-self frequenting them on occasion. Not on a consistent basis. My life's shortcoming is a lack of consistency. The freedom that you helped me find and appreciate by tying my scarf to that tree branch, I still haven't found anything useful to do with it. I'm living free.

I love the atmosphere inside casinos. I sometimes go there. I possess enough money that I don't ever need to win, and I take pleasure in being able to lose a little bit from time to time. I mostly go there to observe the faces of the gamblers.

They're no different than the faces of the blessing-seekers I saw in your lakou. They have all the same anxieties and the same hopes. Yes, I've also sometimes debased myself with a man or a woman in a hotel that charges by the hour. The rooms are not as comfortable as my apartment, or the chic hotels to which I'm often invited. But the partners with whom I choose to shed my clothes express an urgency of desire that pleases me. I often walk the streets alone, stopping at a bar for a drink or a coffee. I catch eyes following me, and I recognize in their expressions a probing sense of chance that, for me, has become a necessity. So, sometimes I give in.

I would have liked to have shared dinner and the tranquility of the coastal plain with you one evening. I recall the scene so often that it's become almost like a dream. I hear you tell me that part of my destiny was to be admired. I believe you and I have accepted this fate. Yet, in my childhood, I was far from being considered a beautiful person. People reproached me for having boney shoulders. I suffered for my looks. It was only later that whispers of admiration took the place of mockery. I was a virgin and embarrassed to be the subject of all the attention. I married my husband because our marriage was convenient for our families, but also because I believed his authoritative eyes liberated me from everyone else's. However, they still followed me. This was when he decided the two of us would need to resort to your services. Pardon this dreadful expression, "resort to your services." It's a reflex. I'll admit that I had never heard of you before. I was more in tune with what went on in the large European cities. Small towns, much like the countryside were, for me, foreign entities. I thought my husband had lost his mind. But I accepted. To please him.

Pleasure, I had never experienced it before in our love life and he resented me for it. The frigid beauty, that's what I called myself. So, the frigid beauty followed her husband who wanted you to bless this scarf, to protect her from the stares of others.

I don't believe in the spirits, nor magic. I don't know how you knew he was going to die. He was a man full of projects and vigor. I'll never cease to thank you on his behalf. He was full of anxiety as well. He tried so hard to respect the family tradition of power and success that he forgot how to experience joy. That final day, in that little hotel in Jérémie, I loved the way he looked at me. Until that moment, I had only ever been his wife. His beautiful wife. On that day, he looked at me without seeing himself. My existence became separate from his own. He looked at me as if he discovered who I was. He was happy and I was free. His joy did not last long. I often think of him and the things we discover when it's too late. My freedom, I take it with me everywhere. I don't fret over the stares. I choose what merits attention, a reaction. At worst, all I risk is a little boredom. But, now that I am in full possession of myself, I never experience fear or disgust. A great painter once asked for permission to paint my portrait. I gave it to him. If people can experience joy by seeing me naked, what do I have to lose? You told me that nobody, nothing must be used to hide beauty. To hide beauty is to appropriate it for own use. So then beauty deserves to be shared like everything else. I think I'm becoming a little bit of a socialist...

I hope to return to my country one day. What prevents my returning is my distaste for wandering. I do not wish to return to the past from whence I came. If I come back, it must be for the whole country. To find a place of my own. As I wait, I'd like to do something to benefit a child. I thought of little Hortense. I can still see her, puckish, tying my scarf to the branch. Would you send me news of her? I bought a corn pipe for you. I wouldn't dare send it.

With my thanks,
E.

Antoine of Gommiers
SECOND APPENDIX

My dear uncle,

i'm asking for your forgiveness for this letter and the bad things that i've done. i was a little girl and, even though the men in the lakou looked at my breasts a bunch, i had already climbed every tree. so, when the lady's money arrived, i disobeyed your order to share it with the others, i jumped on a bus headed to Port-au-Prince.

i'll spare you the misery, the hard times. it's all my fault. Jean went looking, and so Jean found, that's what we say. many time i wanted to return to Gommiers, but i was too ashamed. today i'm pregnant. If it's a boy, he'll be Antoine, if it's a girl, i'll call her Antoinette. i'm writing on her behalf, or on his. to ask you for protection. my mistakes are not their mistakes.

every day i will speak of your name to my child. and of the trees. and the plains. a child must know their roots in this difficult life.

in the city your name is well-known. habits are a vice and i walk with my head in the clouds, i look toward the tree-tops. a man told me: if you continue like that, what i see for you, not even Antoine of Gommiers will have seen. i felt a thousand women within me, an immense strength. but i didn't dare admit you were my oncle. i'm so ashamed.

they tell me you're very ill. division has started to infil-trate the lakou. that's not good. i hope you get better, to restore the order.

say hello to the mapou and the acacias for me

respè
H

I found the letters in a large manila envelope full of newspaper clippings. The first was typed with a typewriter, apart from the initial. The second, written by hand, on yellowed notebook paper in nearly illegible handwriting. I have no idea why Franky took the time to rewrite the letters in a notebook. The women in the alleyway reported to me that Savior, the bookseller, came around often the last few days. Like I should be worried. Like they returned from a secret mission I'd given them to warn me about an impending danger. The bookseller, he keeps Franky company. If he comes around often, all the better. The books are what scare them. The books, there are hardly any of them in the alleyway apart from the free copies of the New Testament distributed by the Église de la Dernière Chance. I don't understand the Pastor's Good Lord much better than I do Antoine of Gommiers. The pastor, he hands out the New Testament, but in his sermons, he only cites the Old. And the idea of loving thy neighbor as thyself has never occurred to him. If I believe what Franky has written, Antoine of Gommiers, real or made up, seer or not, he was not evil. That alone is a quality to have. Joanna also stopped by. Twice, the women in the alley tell me. In uniform. Before she headed to her secretary job in an office building. She didn't stick around enough for a sexual encounter. She broke up with Pépé's associate a long time ago. She's engaged to a civil court bailiff for the northern region, and she seemed quite annoyed with the ladies in the alley. What if she only came to thank Franky. He really helped her out when she was a student. In the manila envelope, there are a bunch of letters. With stamps from different countries. In many languages. I recognized English and Spanish. But there are others that I can't make out. There are also letters that look like they were mailed from here. Franky recopied them all. They filled multiple notebooks. Letters and testimonies. The testimonies are even more numerous than the letters. People recounting what Antoine would have done for them at one moment or another. Reading them, this wasn't some man, but a godsend. Where did Franky manage to unearth all this from? He must have hired Savior as a research assistant. When he came back from Gommiers, in addition to fruit, his bag contained letters. But not this many. These damn letters, these testimonies, they're a mystery. Well, one of the letters proves that Grandma Hortense was not one of Antoinette's inventions. The other letter was about a very wealthy and beautiful woman, traveling the world and not sure of what to do with herself, who made peace with her body since the death of her husband. The testimonies, they prove that people felt better after their visit to Gommiers. It's all about feeling better. Especially since you have no idea how long it'll last. Antoinette and all the women in the alley are burdened women. Burdened by children, obligations, husbands who could care less about anything other than beating on them and giving them more children. I love the idea of this "unburdened" woman. With money do with as she pleases, without having to worry about a screaming child or a man who needs sex. Not bad. An "unburdened" woman. Antoinette, she never belonged to herself. If you love a woman, as a mother or a wife, you must imagine her by herself. Why should work be the source of a woman's happiness? I would've liked Antoinette to experience happiness without servitude. A little bit like Doriane felt after her stepfather left. After Doriane, there were other women. In our memory, she remains the prettiest of all. She's the one who asked us to never come back. Because of our age. We looked too much like a love triangle. She had already become a businesswoman and didn't want to become a kid again. With us, she laughed too much. Together we hummed along to the popular songs. We behaved like kids. Doriane taught us how to leave our childhood behind, and we ran the risk of bringing her back into hers. We also got to know a few real pros. That's it. I don't know if anything happened between Franky and Joanne, the young girl who came to solicit his help with her homework. As for me, something has been known to happen once or twice between myself and female customers. One of them thought that the drawing was rigged and, once in bed, that I would tell her the winning numbers. The drawings are often rigged, but I don't have the numbers. As for the others, perhaps there was an attraction that had nothing to do with numbers. But it never lasts. The two women in our lives are Antoinette and Doriane. A mother and a prostitute who didn't want to become a lover. Old age and the end of innocence.

Testimony of the man who beat his head against the wall:
Until the age of fifteen, I beat my head against the wall. I started as a child, when I could barely walk. At first it was just at home, then at school. Then everywhere. It could happen at any given moment, any given place. I ran towards a wall and gave it a big headbutt. My forehead was a mixture of bumps and scrapes. One day, my parents took me to see an old man. He said to me: "You don't like walls. This is a good instinct. But you're looking at it the wrong way." He took me in front of a little house a few meters away from his own. Walking, we could see an immense coastal plain, with blue at the end of it that must have been the sea. Then he made me stand with my head touching the wall and he said to me, "The wall is keeping you from noticing the coastal plain and the sea. So, what must you do to find them?" That was the day I understood that, in order to overcome an obstacle, to avoid it, or to destroy it, you needed to see the thing standing behind it. The coastal plain, the sea, or something else you can reach out for. I still hate barriers. But I learned how to see beyond them.

There are dozens like this, with titles. From every social class, of all ages. Successes and failures. Simple folk and layabouts. Hardened people, too. Or those who thought they were, with chinks all in their armor. *Testimony of the prison guard: My whole life, I made sure that the people were where they were supposed to be according to society's verdict—in their cells, or busy breaking stones. The Cacos under the Occupation. The petty thieves waiting too long for a trial that never took place. A few murderers. Lots of poor people. Less frequently, the rich who bought their privileges. And men who developed political ideas and promoted social change in opposition to the government. These men, they often entered never to leave. And when they left, it was only to return. I was the prison guard for two thousand three hundred and fifty-one people. One hundred and twenty-five of them died in their cells. Thirteen in the infirmary. Three in the prison yard, during their rec time. When I went into retirement, noticed that all my friends had fled the country. My wife had left me. My children made lives for themselves and had children I've never met. My oldest acquaintances no longer invited me into their homes. I asked to be reintegrated into society. But my seat had been taken. I went to see Antoine of Gommiers to ask him what I should do with the time I had left. Listening to him, I came to realize that only those whom you imprison can liberate you from your solitude. I went back to my empty house, and ever since, I've been naively drawing the faces of those I remember. I hang them on the walls. We talk about this and that. I've already drawn one hundred and fifty-nine faces. There's still plenty of space on the walls. I left the house to my grandchildren I've never met, under the condition that they never take down the portraits.*

Dozens. I don't always understand these stories or the lessons we're supposed to learn from them. I only read a handful of them. Franky writes what he writes because that's who he is. The rest... These days, he and I are all alone. Or, rather, I'm alone with him. Or the only one who takes care of him. Danilo left. For Chile or Brazil. He'll never tell me again: "Kolonn, there's a house to paint. A trick to play. Just to earn a little something extra." Franky, throughout our childhood, he had Maître Cantave to escape real life and travel through the past. I had Danilo.

For the listeners and reporters at Métro-Machin, us, the alley, we're one in the same. They only talk about us in the plural. For them, poverty is our identity. They believe we all have the same relationship to things and that we all take a piss at the same time. When we were kids and the rain was really coming down—since the water would flow through the gutters into the house anyway—we went into action and ran outside naked to play at the entrance of the alley. Franky cried in Antoinette's dirty skirts. Pépé and his gang were already capable of the most heinous violence. The other kids who attended the private institution Le Savoir, with their airs, their petty personal truths that never related to my own. Danilo is the only person like me that I've ever met. The only friend I've grown up with, learned with, and shared things with. He's my brother in the street and in creative spirit. Franky already lived in the past, where there's no price to pay. Everything is free. You can choose your side, assume your point of view, develop your hypotheses, chose the path you'll follow, and shuffle along as you please without any consequences. The enemies and partisans are dead, and their honor and disgrace, their pantheons, and their mass graves have no effect on your everyday life. Starvation is something else. Starvation makes the harmless child want to beat the living shit out of you because going hungry makes people mean. So we wind up taking it out on the closest creature we can find. A dog passing by. Another child. Ourselves sometimes. There was Pacheco, he mutilated himself. His mother thought the devil came into the house at night and lacerated her son's arms and legs. The pastor at the Église de la Dernière Chance coordinated prayers. Danilo and I knew that Pacheco had had enough of squalor, of his uncertain future, and because he lacked the strength to die once and for all, every night he sliced away at another part of his body, extracting from it a little bit of flesh with a razor blade hidden under his mattress. We were the only ones who knew. We threatened to kill him for real if he kept up his nonsense. "And what woman will want you, one day, when you're old enough to have sex, if you have scales like a lizard!" It worked. Though we were no Antoine of Gommiers, Danilo and I had our own brand of wisdom. Our special way of doing things. To pay the price of the present. The present is expensive, it eats up your time. It leaves a mark on you. Danilo paid for it. His stepfather branded him with a hot iron to teach him discipline. Yet, he didn't harbor any hatred. Danilo was my friend, and I was his. In short, together we learned how to be children in a present that has us all by the throat. How to make it. How to make a stand. How to get by. How to make do. How to do without. Danilo's mother preferred his stepfather who abused the two of them. Maybe that's what brought us together, we were nobody's favorite. He was there, a living shadow. When Maître Cantave's praises roused the anger of the jealous kids toward Franky who never learned how to work with his fists. When I left school for the streets to earn my share of the money to help Antoinette. Then, Antoinette's death and Franky's accident. In addition to all his odd jobs, Danilo was my agent. My manager. My bag of tricks to feed two mouths. And the voice to tell me: "Hey, kolonn, even though Franky doesn't get out much, he needs a new shirt." Franky this, Franky that. And Danilo was there to help me pick out the shirt. Yet Franky, lost in his delirium and his papers, was never too friendly with Danilo. Franky needs his friends to be people who don't exist or, at least, haven't existed for a while, and who talk differently than we do. I had a burden and an accomplice. A brother and a companion. The burden remains. The accomplice took a flight to Chile or Brazil. The brother needs a chair. He rots in a chair that won't budge. When he wanted to galivant off on a new adventure, Danilo would come wait for me at the bank at closing time, and he asked to go in it together. Danilo was one of the alley's true geniuses. The person who taught me how to survive. He always found a solution. Laughing along the way. Antoinette was only ever good at peddling her wares and dreaming. Franky... Danilo was all I ever needed. Useful. Free of charge. Efficient. This is the first time he's ever thrown himself into an adventure without inviting me along for the ride. But I can't hold it against him. He's not the one who betrayed me. He didn't ask me out of protection. Maybe I would have wanted to leave, too. I would have hesitated, thinking about Franky. Hesitation brings on sadness. It splits you in two. The two halves fix themselves in opposing directions. You argue back-to-back. After, when you manage to choose, when you cut one out in favor of another, you're no less sad. The losing side never gives up, it wears you down on the inside, and never ceases to remind you that you made the wrong choice. If Danilo said nothing to me, his silence was protective, his way of keeping me from splitting my mind in two. Now, he's no longer here, and I've got to keep my mind together to find a chair for Franky. I have no clue what he'd say about it, their damn Antoine of Gommiers. But during someone's lifetime, we don't always know their name. For all these years, Danilo helped me be there for Franky. "Sorry, kolonn, I forgot to say thanks." He found a passport and a visa for someplace I don't know. I didn't ask him which name is written on the passport or how much he had to pay for it. Here, fake papers can sometimes cost less than real ones. And even if they cost more, you won't spend your whole life waiting for them. "I'm sorry about the name. The news we get from Chile or Brazil isn't always good. On the radio when they'll talk about a suicide or an accident, an act of violence towards one of our own, I'll ask myself if it isn't you. It's true that in terms of making it on your own there's no one better than you. But how will you know if the tricks that work here work somewhere else! Sure, between you and me, we did so many things together and we never told one another thanks. Whatever your new name is, take care of yourself, my friend. Thanks."

Testimony of a man found too ugly to accompany the most beautiful woman in the world: One time I got into a fight with a fellow in the street who asked my fiancée why such a beautiful woman would show her face with a man so ugly and visibly unfortunate? I pretended not to hear a thing. We were walking up a hill. I was walking her back to her house, at the top of the hill. Once she had closed the door, I quickly walked back down the hill and rushed towards the man standing in front of the bar, chattering with his friends. The brawl did not turn in my favor. The noise drew the attention of the neighbors. And I saw her standing at the top of the hill, watching me from the front of her house. Afterwards, I no longer dared to ask her out. When I wanted to rekindle things, she is the one who refused. I felt like the whole world had convinced her, her parents, the people milling in the street, her friends, ultimately proving them right, she had decided to leave me to my ugliness. Antoine of Gommiers saved me from my foolishness. He told me that I had to climb back up that hill, gently knock on her door, and ask for her forgiveness. Forgive me for having placed other peoples' views of others above hers. And, along the way, I had to stop in front of the little bar where the man who stuck his nose in places where it did not belong spent every evening with his friends, and thank him for having recognized the beauty of the woman I loved.

I don't have the heart to read this gibberish. It's too blue. Too rose-colored. Franky's chair no longer works. Danilo told me he knew how to find a new one, for free. But he left without giving me the details. When you leave the alley to make a life somewhere else, it's always done in a rush. And without looking back. The alley is no Sodom. We're not rich, nor peaceful, and with all our activities combined, we don't really fuck that much either. But you decide to leave, if you make the mistake of looking back, a cinderblock will fall on your head, a tap tap's brakes will fail, a child, a brother, a friend. At closing time at the bank, Danilo wasn't the one there waiting for me. It was Savior. The ladies in the alley were right. I should have suspected it. I started walking without really listening to him. Savior has a voice that creeps along. Just like his feet. This pesky voice that comes from his nose. A trap. I walked on. Stalked by a voice and a pair of legs creeping behind me. Wanting to catch up with me. Attract my attention. Not the time, my friend. My mind has to stay straight, focused on the reality at hand. Stick to my goal: find a chair. He chased me down. Scurrying as fast as possible. His nasally voice. A sort of whistling. A persiflage. He wanted some money. "I've done so many things for Franky." Lots of things, perhaps. But next week is payday. And it won't even cover the chair. I kept walking and he continued to follow me, shouting my name "Listen... Ti Tony... For Franky... For real, so much." More important than his wheelchair? Give me a fucking break. My mind is working. Working for two. And Martine will still grumble before handing me the plates of food. I'm behind by two months. Thursdays cost twice as a much because of the lambi in place of stew. Franky doesn't like stew. Not the time to prattle on with an old bookseller. "Franky said you'd understand. I was thinking, if you gave me the winning numbers for the next drawing, call it a down payment. I helped him out because I like his project. But there comes a time when you have to mix work with pleasure, and the work is severely lacking." I turned around. Goddammit, enough about Franky! "How would I know! Don't you think that if I had the winning numbers, I would've placed a bet on money that I don't have! Isn't that what you did? I started walking again. Savior is old. It's spiteful, but it calmed me down to force him to run. His bag chock-full of old books or some other crap weighted him down, and he was out of breath. "Cons. All kinds of cons. The stamps. The yellowing paper. The calligraphy. The newspaper cuttings. I held onto sources and contacts. Besides, I'm the one who hooked your friend Danilo up with the contacts for his passport. I know about all sorts of cons." I stopped to snatch him up by the shirt collar. I'm going to fuck you up, you and your phonies. And don't get Danilo caught up in your bullshit." He trembled. You never hit a trembling old man, even if behind his trembling you notice he's hiding the smile of a con artist. It's a trick. Just like the little kid who stranded us in the filthy waters of Port-au-Prince. Trapped once again by the appearance of goodness. I thought that Savior was freely passing books Franky's way, out of affection for the lone reader in the alley. "Franky, he's happy." And the words of the little kid came back to me. "The king, and you'll work in service of the king." And what if I was tired of being in service to the king? Savior wouldn't give up. "Franky… He's done. By the time we realize we've been hoodwinked, folks will start to believe it. When lies are out in the open and find an audience, they have the value of truth. He said that you'd understand. Anyway, someone had better pay me. You see, out of pleasure I played my part. Now, someone has to take care of the work." There's only one person to pay for the king's bullshit: me. And I don't want to anymore. Without apologizing, or looking at him either, or listening to him. I picked up the pace. He kept following me. Desperation can speed things up. Hauling himself faster than my anger, he got in front of me. His bag fell to the ground. Instinctively, I picked it up. Fuck you, Antoinette. And your Antoine of Gommiers. Your dead-legged Franky. And your lessons in manners. Defeated, I let him walk along next to me. "What did you do before?"

"Accountant, in the public sector. An investigator responsible for verifying documents for the Ministry of Justice. I was only a petty crook. I forged documents for poor people. They took me up on it. The big guns kept on working for the big guns and never caught wind of it. Savior isn't my real name. All the client had to do was ask. And I'd get what he wanted. Technically, I was the best. It wasn't just for the money. What's true, what's false, sometimes it's only a matter of power. You see? Work and pleasure. Tricking people for a worthy cause, isn't it as good as sin?" An old con artist. Asking me for money, full of ideas. What the hell has gotten into everyone, philosophizing! And what am I going to do about the chair? Your boss, did you notice he's almost rooted to the spot? "Get lost. I can't promise you anything." —"Thanks." —"Get lost and don't say thanks. I can't promise you a thing." He left. Without forcing the issue. Contenting himself with this half-promise. "Wait. One final question. Danilo, what'd he put on his passport?" —"I have no idea what you're talking about." —"What name did he use?" —"I don't know. Tony, I think. Tony something."

Testimony of the prostitute wanting to return to her child-hood. *From the boy who fell from a roof one Sunday. From the woman who played every time but never won. From the woman who wanted to live life lying down. From the good man wanting to pass as someone mean. From the petty lottery salesman who spends his life looking after his brother. From the forger-in-chief. From the faithful friend.*

"You're insane. All this bullshit, you made it all up. And how am I supposed to pay Savior what we owe him! We barely have enough to buy a wheelchair. Hardly enough for our food." He was right there. Vulnerable but calm as I shouted. It was the first time the neighbors heard shouting between us. And they were already crowded together outside the door. "Danilo's gone, that's what's making you so upset. You would've liked for it to be me. But, don't you see, I'd like to go somewhere else, too, but I can't. Except to the cemetery." His hand stretched out towards mine. The king wanting to bring peace to his subject. "We'll find a publisher." —"What's a publisher?" And he started explaining it to me. And, for the first time, it was like he was lecturing me. For the first time, it was too much nonsense. "Who would waste their time and money to publish this piece of shit!" Goddammit! Why didn't he learn how to walk on a roof like all the rest of us around here, how to use a paintbrush and a hammer, how to do it yourself, avoid a punch, how to throw a jab and an uppercut, how to steal electricity, instead of wallowing in the past with that show-off Cantave and his elements of style, his lot of useless extended metaphors, increasing and decreasing gradations, hyperboles and I don't even know what. Shit! Here, you learn to get by. You're not supposed to get your hair caught in a fucking cable, and smash your kidneys on the edge of the sidewalk to lock yourself away in a nasty bedroom in a wheelchair that no longer has wheels to write nonsense about a so-called seer whose predictions have nothing to do with your miserable existence. I lost it, I pushed his hand away and opened the suitcase to pour out its contents, throwing everything behind me. *Treatise on Style, The Art of Memoir Writing, The Relationship between History and Legends, Things Seen and Heard in the Peninsula of Grand Anse, The Mysteries of Haiti...* bounced off the wall before scattering all over the floor. He wanted to stop me. He tried to stand up. He managed to for about a second. I saw him standing. In my face. Right in front of me. Pitted against me. His arms, stronger than I had imagined them to be, as strong as my own, dragging me to the ground. Then he crumpled. His legs sending the chair crashing against the table. And all his pages fell to the ground, together with the books. The backdated letters. The forged stamps. the false testimonies. The bus companies, *Griffonnes* and *Jérémiades*. The newspaper "Ad libitum." The blue herons. The master's two secretaries and their sons. Little Hortense who loved to climb trees. And in the bunch of papers, among these things true and false sprawled out in disorder, among these banal occurrences to which he had wanted to bring meaning, to illuminate, sat the photo of two boys dressed like cowboys on a wooden horse, their resemblance so close that, in order to distinguish between the two, their mother had written their first initial on the front of their hats.

I helped him back up into his chair. I put the books back into his briefcase. I gathered the papers from the floor and put them in front of him on his table. He started to organize them. I watched him, sitting in my half of the room. He ensured that the pages were in their proper place, and he put them together in a large manila envelope. He didn't appear surprised when I took the envelope. I went outside to smoke my daily cigarette. The doors and windows were still open outside. A dispute between Franky and me, that was a first. Folks must have been sad that it didn't last long. In the alley, you can't resist a novelty. Something that alters the usual cycle of violence. I wanted to do my Danilo impression and shout that if they stuck their noses where they didn't belong then I'd divulge all the ladies' sexual secrets. But they wouldn't buy it. The alley is a tiny little world, and everyone who lives there has known for a while what everyone is capable of. A small world where, even if at any moment life causes us to betray our nature, adapt and become someone else, there are still extremes that we fail to reach.

We remain more or less the same. Danilo flirted with gangs, but that didn't last long. Franky busted his kidneys when he tried to walk on rooftops. You may adopt new identities, you become the other that you can. I cannot act like Danilo. Life is like in that play he saw at the Rex. Two beggars, after arguing with one another for the nth time, swearing to separate. They could keep their word. Life, it pushes you around, changes you, changes some more, and then, just like that, you revert to the person you were all along. Even if your name isn't Fatal. Fatal, where did that asshole of an author find a name like that? I asked myself that very question, then I started walking toward the Cité.

The sons of the secretaries maintain that, feeling the effects of old age, Antoine of Gommiers sometimes gathered the inhabitants of the lakou to converse with them about a given theme. It could be something light, even frivolous to those who thought themselves wiser than the master and expected more seriousness on his behalf. Seafoam. The ears of a donkey. Things to which people hardly paid attention and the existence of things from which one does not ordinarily draw a lesson or an important principle. Antoine of Gommiers also expressed himself on more abstract and vital things, symbols of the human condition which could manifest themselves for good or evil in anyone. Patience and anger came up often. The master taught that in every respect, one should not confuse things with their appearance. And that, above all, from feelings to actions, from the greeting of a passerby to the simplest of our gestures, the value of things depends only on their use. And so, patience. When we leave time to time itself, and it is not lost, time allows things to evolve into their true selves. Time is only wasted when fear justifies an immovable stagnation that prevents us from seeing, loving, and comprehending the things before us if we have the strength to make a leap or the intelligence of a child to sit down and enjoy something for a short while. Anger, too. The master condemned anger when it was nothing more than the expression of wounded vanity, and, to the surprise of the elderly, he praised when it sanctioned a deliberate intention to constrict life. He himself displayed during these conversations a great patience towards his interlocutors, particularly for the adults, slower to express themselves than the children and sometimes getting tangled up in mediocre and pointless considerations. Sometimes, tired of repeating the same things to people officially at the age of comprehension, he left the children in charge of the exchange and fell asleep under the soursop tree—his face half smiling, half angry.

Triangle was seated in the front next to the driver, Speedy.
Speedy only loves one thing, driving. He never talks when
he's behind the wheel. Pépé appreciates his silence and made
him his personal driver. The seat was too small for Triangle,
and he wiggled himself to find a more comfortable position.
I was sitting in the back, on the driver's side. The passen-
ger's side, that was the boss's seat. Speedy parked the car in
the courtyard of the Society. We got out, Triangle, Pépé, and
me. The security guard on duty in the courtyard asked what
brought us here. At this time the Society's building was closed
to the public. The only person left inside was the receptionist tidying up her desk, ready to leave. We watched her busy
herself through the bay windows. The guard glanced at the
baton hanging from his hip. His eyes fixed on Triangle, it
was a quick evaluation to conclude that, in the face of such
a monstrosity, it was not a weapon they had given him, but
a toy. "Alright, come on in." The receptionist was standing,
organizing files, her bag sitting on the desk. "We're closed."

Her head lowered. "We wish to see the President." Finally, eye contact. Remembering that at the secretarial school they had taught her the art of affability. Even with visibly uneducated strangers smelling of cheap perfume and a blend of fragrances from a bath of leaves. A pretty girl. Intent on being pretty and polite. She consulted her watch, resigning herself to act the part for a few minutes longer. She smiled affably. At the secretarial school, they must have prepared her for the possibility of unforeseen circumstances and overtime. She produced another affable smile. She was a really pretty girl. Then she saw Triangle and her smile turned into an "Oh," which altered her features, changing her beauty into fear. There shouldn't be giants like Triangle in the same world as researchers. The President wasn't there. The library was closed. And to gain access to the library, you had to fill out a registration form and pay the small subscription fee. Thanks for the information. Would the President be coming back? No, he went back home to his house in the heights, in Péguy-Ville. "That's a long way." Could we have his address? "The thing is... I don't know..." She winked desperately at the security guard standing outside. He pretended not to notice her, finally turning away so as to not have to continue pretending. She dared to ask the question, forcing herself to salvage her beauty and her smile to ask. "May I ask to what this visit pertains?" She looked like Joanna when she did her practice exercises with Franky. I did my Franky impersonation. "A piece of history, miss. Why else would we look to see the President of the Historical Society if not to discuss a piece of history?" Clearly, she didn't believe us. Not only because, in the world of Historians, she had never seen one the size of Triangle. But the five rings on Pépé's right hand and the two gold chains around his neck with a skull pendant and a blue cross, respectively, were also a first for her. I showed her the manila envelope containing the manuscript. The sight of the envelope reassured her a little. After all, we're packing paper. An envelope, a manuscript. Two things she was used to that were never threatening. "For the submission of manuscripts, that's only done on Mondays. And you will have to fill out the submission form." Pépé's response: "We can't wait till Monday." He agreed to help me out. But the offer was only valid for today. Pépé: "It's urgent." Fear once again. She must have encountered people like this before, lunatics who brought in their manuscripts in which they claimed to have uncovered absolute truths. None of this caliber. Apart from a few gestures of exasperation or desperation, authors who think they're unsung geniuses must not pose much of a threat. Franky had advised Joanna to remain calm in every situation. A good receptionist must know how to keep calm under all circumstances, marshalling flexibility and firmness, always in control. Without realizing it, she heeded Franky's advice. To salvage her calm demeanor and demonstrate an interest, cajoling her adversary, and a third smile: "What is it about?" —"The past, miss. What else would you expect a manuscript we've just submitted to the President of the Historical Society to be about? The history of Grand Anse, would you like for us to tell you more?" I actually liked putting on my Franky impression, it added an element of style. "No, that's not necessary. As far as the content goes, I'm not the one doing the judging. That's the prerogative of the members of the Society. —"It's not the President who decides?" —"Yes, when it's all said and done, but he appreciates when all the members give their opinion." I was not mistaken. A democratic President. The kind of President with the patience to listen to everyone's opinion before developing his own thesis. The receptionist, slightly relieved, asked me: "Are you the author?" —"Not at all. I don't know how to write. I'm only a messenger." Pointing to Triangle: "Him, he's the author." Panic once more. The author's huge. And, Pépé added: "With the hands you see here," talking to Triangle, "show her your hands." The author's mitts were huge. Capable of engulfing the receptionist's beautiful face by themselves. I heard her thinking about it. These hands were made for wreaking havoc, not for writing. But she must have been educated at a truly exceptional school and recruited by the competition. A fourth smile. Exactly the same as the previous three. The school didn't teach the other variations of a smile. She scrawled the address on a piece of paper. Holding out her hand. Daring not to hand it to the author. Triangle's hands are so big and fat that one might be afraid of getting lost in them. She chose me as the one she would hand the piece of paper. If our intentions were to harm the President, she could defend herself. "The address, I gave it to the one who seemed the least dangerous to me." That annoyed me. Without having the soul of a killer, there are times when you'd like for other people to think you're dangerous enough not to get on your bad side. A lot of things would have been quicker, and that would spare us circumlocutions. Another word Franky cherished. It can be so annoying to always have words of three or more syllables shoved in your face all the time. The receptionist was happy to witness the end of the conversation. Happy to go home and kick off her shoes. Joanna, what she hated the most in her comportment exercises she practiced with Franky, was having to confine her rather beautiful feet in shoes. "Well, best of luck."—"Thank you, miss." For the address and your smile. Go home and unleash your feet. Especially if they're beautiful. Antoine of Gommiers said... Here I was, letting myself be convinced by Franky's ramblings... Once at the door, we heard the secretary with the conventional smile, whose feet might be killing her, chew out the security guard. At school, perhaps they taught her that smiles are useful for visitors, but not for underlings. The guard, without having budged from his spot in the courtyard, raised his arms and hands much smaller than Triangle's meat hooks to demonstrate his impotence.

The stories vary. Antoine of Gommiers died, some say, on the wild beach of Gommiers after his swim, surrounded by shore birds. Others recount that one afternoon he did not awaken from his nap. The children seated at his feet awaiting the future, troubled by his silence and the blood dripping from his mouth, grabbed his hat and went to alert the adults. Still others say that, disappointed by the factions warring beneath the surface of the lakou about the redistribution of land and property rights, he turned away from his loved ones after one final glimpse toward the children, laid down in his bed and entered into eternity through the gates of sleep. After his passing, there was nothing about the war that lay beneath the surface. Brought to machete blows and poisonings, the war would not come to an end until there was nothing left to share apart from a few fruit-bearing trees and a few iron-sick, cankerous resin harvesters. Folks still say that his revelations affected him physically. His knowledge of the future had worn down his legs and his organs. Towards the end, he who consumed very little to begin with, hardly ate a thing. He struggled to make it to the end of his blessing ceremonies. That was when everyone realized they could not say how old he was and that even the divine are not eternal. The master would, quite simply, die of old age. An ordinary death, natural, banal, hardly worthy of his stature.

Apart from some exceptions, death reminds us of our shared condition, which we can pretend to escape by the merit of our actions and the brilliance of our reputations. Death can betray life, uncertain of the memory people will hold of our passing, our last wish can be to erase its very traces. Knowing this, Antoine of Gommiers had, before his death, dismissed his two secretaries and, according to the recollections of the first secretary's son, burned the notebook in which he recorded the names of all his illustrious visitors. The son of the second secretary restated that Antoine did not possess a register, and he simply asked to be buried in his white suit, his hat resting in his hands, deciding that this would be the final image he hoped people would retain of him.

If we understand the idea a person has of themselves by analyzing their last requests, there too, mystery hangs over the personality of the man from Gommiers. In most cases, the evidence of symbolism leaves no room for doubt. Such a man might have wished, selfish until his death, to see his wife that he supposedly loved to return every evening for the rest of her life, dressed in black, to kneel at the foot of his tomb and mourn his absence. We can conclude that there is boundless vanity, going so far as to demand post-mortem fidelity from a veiled subordinate. Another man might have wished to once again see the neighborhood where he grew up, a landscape, a *body, a painting. We can deduce that he desired to go out in style, his eyes open to a happy period of his life or the most beautiful image on which he would ever feast his eyes.*

Antoine of Gommiers would have, according to some, foretold and prepared his own resurrection. He only had to open his coffin, stand up, and greet his audience with a tip of his hat. One misstep by his sons in conducting the ritual, one word said in the place of another, could bar him access to the miracle and rattle the faith of the disappointed crowd. Should we give the slightest credit to this fable, closer to a carnivalesque mysticism than the wisdom that the sage from Grand Anse had demonstrated all his life? According to others, under the guise of a last supper he only ate a handful of dirt and wild grass, carrying with him in his stomach a sliver of his first love, this coastal plain he had cherished. The editor-in-chief and owner-publisher of the newspaper "Ad Libitum" prided himself in announcing the passing of "a small, noteworthy figure, a true son of Grande-Anse," of whom it could not be said whether he had been a "charlatan or a genius blessed with a presocratic wisdom," and "to whom certain government officials, known for their incompetence, had incurred a few debts." This time, the Minister of Public Works chose not to respond. He had just learned about his latest appointment to the post of Minister of Religious Cults and already applied the approach of his future ministry regarding everything that related to ancestral and religious beliefs: silence.

Just because you can't read, doesn't mean you have to be rude. Pépé ordered Speedy to drop us off at a bar-restaurant and return to home base to commandeer another vehicle. We weren't going to Péguy-Ville in a rickety bucket of bolts. Triangle hoped to stay with the boss, but Pépé told him it wasn't necessary. He wanted to spend some time with an old classmate. The expression, so foreign to his personality, felt out of place coming from his mouth. My surprise wounded him. His eyes said it all. He went there all the same, to the private institution Le Savoir. Even when we knew him when we were little, we tend to believe that killers have no past. I knew Pépé when he was only a dunce who broke the tip of his pencil, pressing down too hard on the piece of paper. That was, incidentally, why we found ourselves in a normal bar-restaurant. Nothing luxurious, but not run-down either. Yes, that must be it, the norm. A middle ground between not rich and not poor. An average bar. With average people. With enough money to buy themselves the daily special, have a drink or two, and return to the monotony of their normal lives. Prices more expensive than those in the Cité or even on Grand Rue, but a far cry from the ones in play in the President's neighborhood. We sat ourselves down at a table in the back, with Pépé choosing the seat from which he could see the entrance. "Do you buy it, Franky's "memoir? And what does that even mean, a memoir?"—"I don't know. I didn't learn a whole lot. I'm..."

I was about to say "just like you" but I stopped myself before I could finish my sentence. "You can say it. But you're not like me. You didn't want to be. You decided to leave knowledge to Franky. You wanted to be Franky's protector. Me, all this stuff went over my head. But do you believe it, his memoir about the life of Antoine of Gommiers?"—"I have no idea. I sell lottery tickets to folks who buy their chances of winning and lose every day. History, Antoine of Gommiers, all these debates about the past and the future, it's not my thing. I'm just doing this for Franky." It was mostly couples, the bar's clientele. Of average age. Of average social standing. Low-level workers, as we say. Nothing about us said low-level. A little gang boss and an employee at a bòlèt bank. But little, not so much; Pépé must have had enough money in his pockets to pay for everyone's meal. Even more. A whole lot more. One of the couples didn't look happy. You could feel the tension between them. From time to time, the man violently squeezed the woman's wrist. We each ordered a beer. The server looked at Pépé's rings and handed him his beer, retreating slightly. Pépé smiled. He enjoys it, scaring people. "Franky has always been a little fragile. Too many ideas. One time, when I received an average grade on a composition. I asked him to re-write it for me. He hesitated. I convinced him to do it by threatening to cut off one of your fingers. Cantave knew too well that I wasn't the author. He reproached Franky for getting mixed up with a dunce doubled as a thug. Franky never confessed and Cantave punished him." Franky never told me. Since childhood, he prefers not to talk about the here and the now. I had been stupid to think that it's because he wasn't aware of it all. – "Would you have done it?"—"What?" — "Cut off one of my fingers?" — "No. Not back then. Later on, no doubt. When I understood, in the alley, the only way to assert yourself is to say things that scare people and then to do what you say. I learned that. And that humiliation was worse than suffering. Before I became the boss, I practically had to wipe the boss's ass. The lieutenants didn't give a shit about me. I killed the boss. But before I did, I humiliated him. One day, it'll happen to me. Some young buck will kill me after humiliating me." The tone of the conversation deteriorated between the nervous couple. The man raised his voice. We could barely hear the woman's voice, who spoke with her head lowered. The whimpering of a wounded dog. The man was no longer satisfied with squeezing her wrists. He shook her by the collar of her shirt and violently pulled her towards him. As though he wanted to drag her over the top of the table. Sobs replaced her whimpering. The other customers seated around them turned towards the couple. The server came over to ask the man to calm down. "Mind your own business. This bitch cheated on me." The wife sobbed even more. The man pulled a card out of his pocket and showed it to the server, who chose to walk away apologizing:

"Sorry, boss." It must have been a police ID or a security guard ID. While continuing to slap the wife around, the man shot threatening glares at the customers and they buried their noses back into their plates of food, pretending to resume their conversations. —"Are you mad at me, about Cantave?" —"I'm not sure if it's us, you, me, other people we should be mad at or whether it's the alley itself. You could have chosen not to kill him. Beyond all his insults, I think he cared about us." —"I think so too. I said it. When you say something, you do it. Otherwise, you're nothing. The rules of the gang are nothing like politics. In politics, the truth doesn't matter. You say things that you'll never do, and you'll still find thousands of morons wanting to re-elect you. He didn't moan. It's the only time I ever respected him. But that's what it's like to be a boss. It's not a matter of good and evil that drives you to do things. Or rarely."

"I don't love you anymore. I want a divorce." The woman lifted her head and shouted. So that the whole dining room could hear. A wounded dog no more. And then came the slap. The man stood up, went to the other side of the table, and grabbed the woman by her hair. The slap, it was just a prelude. On to the serious things. A punch to the stomach. Another to the face. The woman fell. And the foot took over for the fist. Things turned even more serious. Another kick to the stomach. Then the face. As though he could only strike her in the same order. The stomach. Then the face. In gradation. Gradation was one of those elements of style Maître Cantave and Franky liked to use. There were a few, increasing and decreasing, I think. When hitting the woman, the man preferred the increasing kind. Customers rushed toward the exit. Others hung back and watched the spectacle, their backs against the wall. Pépé stood up. He pulled a nine-millimeter from his waistband, fired a shot in the air and shouted: "That's enough." He pointed his hand cannon toward the man who, still standing, started to tremble. Then, still shaking, the man got to his knees. Decreasing gradation. His weapon pointed at the kneeling man, Pépé asked the server to bring him some rope and told the customers to take their seats or leave quietly. The server brought back the rope and Pépé forced him to tie the man to the leg of the table. He said to the woman: "You're free to do what you wish. With him. Or with yourself." It reminded me of the episode with the veil tied to the tree, and the story of this woman with "her beauty restored by Antoine of Gommiers." A beautiful analogy, as Franky is prone to find. A veil and body blows aren't exactly the same thing, and as for the seer and the thug, everyone has their own path. The woman was ashamed and readjusted her torn shirt. You could see her middle-aged breasts. Without looking at the man, she moved toward the exit. Not yet healed from her fear. Suddenly, she made a U-turn, walked over to the man whose back was tied to the leg of the table, his face looking toward the spectacle of which he had been the hero prior to becoming its victim. She kicked him in the teeth, striking with her heel. Then she left. Pépé and I sat back down, his gun resting on the table, and we kept talking for a few minutes longer, before Triangle returned. "Why'd you do that?"—"What, Cantave?" —"No, that," pointing to the man bleeding from the mouth. —"Because there can't be two bosses in one place. And I don't often have the chance to step into action in this part of the city where people think they're better than we are. Because ever since I became the boss, I'm out of practice and I'm in danger of losing my touch. Or, maybe, because once every thousand times, we get the urge to do the right thing." Triangle showed up, understanding everything without any need for explanation. He left a rack on the counter. For the damages and the meal. Without taking off his shoes, he grabbed the man by his pant-legs to remove them. The man was still bleeding. Ridiculous. With his underwear, his skinny legs, red socks. The worst is humiliation. Even worse than destitution. You're alone in your destitution. There's no immediate, omnipotent adversary hanging over your head. You can curse fate, decrying providence. With humiliation, there's someone else telling you you're nothing. It's what the man did to the woman. It's what Pépé and Triangle did to the man. And to many others before him. Just like everyone else, I know about the rapes, the kidnappings, the murders. Pépé and Triangle are not good people. They'll take their mistakes to the grave. A violent death lies in their future. But it didn't bother me, the way they made use of their power. Today. At this very moment. We all have this type of moment where we have the power to reduce the other to nothing. Or to someone. That's what I had done to Franky, despite myself. And Pépé, who had been on both sides of humiliation, was going to help me make amends. Triangle took the wallet out of one of the pants pockets, and he took out the card the man had shown to the server. He pretended to read it. "There, I have your name and address. If anything happens to that woman, what'll happen to you, not even Antoine of Gommiers could have seen coming."

Yes, you can be uneducated without being rude. The vehicle was suitable for the neighborhood. With A/C and automatic everything. The gate was high up. Neither a guard dog nor a security guard. Nothing but a little dog that must have yapped at the slightest breeze. A toy. I'd only seen the President once, on the day Antoinette died. I remember the light in his eyes, the tremors in his hands, this wise old man's affability that welcomed the impatience of the students engulfing his car. A man like him didn't seem like a person who expected people to come all the way to his house with the intent to cause him harm. A sort of luxurious Cantave. Cantave also didn't expect to witness harm, either. These guys are harmless lunatics living in the world's past and their student's future. Knowledge is their universe. When the present comes knocking, they have no clue how to react. We constitute one hell of a disturbance. Triangle and Pépé stayed in the car. Triangle, as soon as you see him, it's straight to fear. There was no need to frighten the President. Fear can be the death of lucidity. And that causes stupid shit to happen. The little toy dog wouldn't stop barking. The President cracked the gate open. Without the slightest suspicion. Simply curious. "Yes?" —"Good evening, Mr. President, I'm here for a consultation." —"It's a little late." Still no suspicion. Just some dignitary, a little upset. "Are you a student?" —"Yes, Mr. President." He was another Maître Cantave, a Cantave from the beautiful neighborhoods. With probably even more knowledge. But the same mannerisms. You only had to say "student" for Cantave to make himself available. "Studying history." —"Ah... But it's still a little late." —"Pardon me, Mr. President. I wouldn't have disturbed you if it weren't an emergency." —"About what?" —"Antoine of Gommiers." He wasn't expecting that one. Disappointed. It wasn't a matter of real history. In the meantime, impatient, Pépé and Triangle got out of the car. And Pépé said, "This could go two ways. Either you invite us inside, or we invite ourselves." The dignitary suddenly grew aware of the reality. Three strangers at his door. A giant, another of average size with all the ornamentation of a gangster on his body, and a smaller one squeezing a large manila envelope. Behind him, the toy wouldn't stop barking. That's it, a salon dog, a little luxury toy that cowers behind its master. The President instead chose to find comfort in the envelope I handed him, on which I had written: *Antoine of Gommiers, A Memoir.* The power of the written word. Words, he was in his comfort zone. Even though, to his surprise, when I told him the reason for our visit, I had understood that Antoine of Gommiers wasn't really a serious subject in his eyes. Or else, reality had left him entirely indifferent. Without any further sign of worry, he opened the gate, turning his back on us. His fragile neck at the mercy of Triangle's meat hooks. He was wearing a bathrobe. A Cantave in a bathrobe. With his skinny ankles and three strangers walking behind him. Maybe he was a man who never lost his cool. We walked through the living room, another room where the TV was turned to a soccer match with English commentary. The President must be a fan and speak many languages. A glass, a bucket of ice, and a bottle of whiskey on a little table. The President must be a fan speaking many languages who drank whiskey alone at night watching soccer matches broadcast in foreign languages. The next room: the library. A domain. His domain. Only then did he turn towards us, as though he was expecting a compliment. In the presence of books, he was no longer this lost little man in a bathrobe too big for his own height. The lightning that sparked in his eyes during the talk the day Antoinette lit herself up. Thousands of books. Bound and well organized. Triangle had never seen books up close before. Pépé, the few he'd seen on the bookshelves at the institution Le Savoir never interested him. Franky probably owns about twenty or so, which he keeps in his suitcase. The President calmly offered us to take a seat. Not wanting to break anything, Triangle wisely chose the sturdiest of the chairs, a mahogany stool, to rest the tip of his butt. Pépé and I sat down on a sofa. "What do you want from me?" —"Your opinion, Mr. President. And a favor." Somewhere in the house, the toy yapped. The toy's ridiculous yapping approached the library. A very beautiful woman opened the door, the toy in her arms. Seeing us, she took a step back. Safe in the arms of its mistress, the toy was particularly bothered by Triangle. He smelled of an overdose of fragrance from baths of leaves. The President reassured the woman. "Everything's alright, my love. I have a work meeting with these gentlemen. Sorry I forgot to tell you about it. Take the dog away, please." The beautiful woman left with the dog. I handed the envelope to the President. Without looking up, he started reading. Like we didn't even exist.

*The elders recounted that upon the announcement of An-
toine from Gommier's death,* the true seers of Grand Anse
impotently invoked the forces governing the fate of mankind.
Conscious of having entered a new era, subject to loss and the
unforeseen, they paid homage to the master, each in their own
way. He who, in kneeling to kiss the soil "you giveth and taketh
away, sowed us paths of fruitful grain and ryegrass, scarci-
ty one day, harvest another." He who, in crossing kilometers
of plains to reach the summit of the highest mountain, lifted
his gaze to the heavens and glimpsed, beyond the clouds, the
promises of tomorrow and the obstacles of the winds of change.
He who, at the simidor's call gathered the inhabitants of his
village at the foot of the mapou in the grand yard, elders and
new-born, infirm and strapping, matrons and young ladies,
launched into a sacred song, long memorized by the chorus:
"Papa Loko, you are the wind, lift our wings, butterflies we
are, and we'll carry the news to Agwe." He who, in confining
himself to silence after extensive self-discussion, pronounced

the inevitable truths of silence and the vanity of songs, sacred or profane.

Every hill has two slopes, every plateau has a low-lying flat, the world is like a notebook in which everything is written, front to back; the elders also recount that the false seers held council and unanimously proclaimed that finally "he had cleared the horizon," a phrase that had been uttered by a scribe thirsting for power and recognition upon the death of a great poet, himself a mystic and adept at divination. But given the council's lack of literary culture, it was better to speak of coincidence rather than plagiarism. The council concluded with defeat, in a fishtail rotten to its guts or maybe without guts at all, each of the nine participants voting for himself as the successor, so that after the ninth round they parted in disappointment, even more divided than during the master's lifetime.

The reading lasted an hour. Two or three times, the President smiled. Twice, he stood up to consult some books, putting them back again in their place. There were thousands of books. But without any hesitation. He knew where to find what he was looking for. After he finished reading, he said: "You're aware that at least half this is fiction? It's a hint of research in service of a fable." An assessment. His face betrayed no feelings. "So, are you going to publish it or not?" No response. Not even a glance toward Pépé, whose attitude was menacing. Pépé and Triangle, that's what they were here for. To apply a little pressure. The problem with the two of them is that when they apply pressure, they try so hard to impose a solution that then very quickly becomes the problem. I didn't want that to happen. I asked for Pépé's help mostly for the money. I think we call that the account of the author in disguise. It was to show the President that we had the money. But the President, the little man in the bathrobe who knew the exact place of every book in his library and could read peacefully in the presence of two thugs who didn't even bother to hide their weapons, if he was aware of a threat, he didn't let on. He seemed to be talking more to himself than to us. "Who's the author?" — "Franky, Mr. President. Franky's my brother. If you ran into him in the street, you'd think it was me. It's crazy how much we look alike. But there are lots of ways in which we're not alike. Whatever. There's little chance you'd ever run into us in the street, me or him. He doesn't go anywhere. I can still walk, but I mostly walk along Grand Rue. The important thing is that Franky, this fable, is all he has to left to make a living for himself. You, being the President that you are, I don't spend my time developing theses or chasing after conference speakers, I'm telling you, your evaluation is that of a learned dignitary. There are times, Mr. President, when the thing you're looking for is a fable. For better or worse. For people living in the alley, there are times when all we leave behind is a fable. Or, to speak your own language, the facts or the details needed to invent a fable. Antoine of Gommiers, a seer or not—what do I give a shit? He was there lying on the ground. Everywhere and nowhere. Especially in poor peoples' homes. Like a threat we can't stop throwing at one another. Poor people, Mr. President, they pick everything up off the ground and throw it right back into your face. So, Franky picked him up. Franky's my brother. Right, I already said that. But I insist so I won't forget. My brother. Who lost his Antoinette and his legs. Who could have become a member and, maybe one day, the President of a society like yours. If he had continued his schooling. If this, if that... Franky's brilliant. Maître Cantave's the one who said it. Brilliant and lonely. Even lonelier than I am. Until last week I had Danilo.

Danilo was my best friend. My right-hand man, and we had a lot of fun together. Franky lives with the dead and his rhetorical devices. And they're all he has to amuse himself with. The dead and rhetoric. He's the only one in the alley who knows what a hypallage is. He tried to explain it to me. But when words are too long and the sentences are too complicated, I doze off and Franky's left talking, all alone. As far as tangible things, he's completely useless with his hands. The last time he wielded a hammer, we were little, and he mistook his thumb for a nail. Antoinette gave me a beating. Franky, he was her favorite, so I had to pay for his awkwardness. Our childhood was like that. Then, when he wanted to imitate us and act like a painter, he caught his head on a cable and abandoned his legs right there. As far as tangible things and everyday life go, he's the epitome of awkwardness. But with words, he has the magic touch. Brilliant, Maître Cantave always used to say. So brilliant that he can put the words in peoples' mouths that they should have said if they had learned how to speak. The things that they should have done if they learned how to act. With words, Franky makes people come alive with words. I mean he gives them a fresh start. A beating heart. Dreams. Feelings. Even accomplishments. I criticized him for not having a vocation. I was wrong. My job is to help Moïse with his accounting. And to fill out tickets for customers. And to find the solution to concrete problems. His job is to sing the blues. Antoinette. The plains. A dog walking by. Give him someone or something, and he'll turn it into something better, irreducible. Hang on, I'm trying to find the right word to describe what he does. That's it, I found it. He gives

them an aspiration. Maybe it's because he doesn't go anywhere except in his own mind. Origin, disaster, aspiration.
That's Franky's style. To go anywhere, to blaze a path, he
needs an origin. An access ramp. So then he brought Antoine of Gommiers back to life. Not to offend you, Mr. President, but nobody in your society of snobs barricaded behind their pulpits, their concepts, and their theses has ever
thought that right there was a patrimony worthy of preser-
vation. No, that's not it. I'm not going to start talking like
you. Or Franky. I don't give a shit about patrimony. I'll leave
that for you to discuss at the next roundtable between you
and your colleagues. How many of your colleagues in this
fucking country and on this fucking earth take the time to
find an aspiration for other people? Antoine of Gommiers is
a name that rolls off peoples' tongues in the plains and in the
alley to announce the worst to come. Franky put words into
his mouth that could be useful. How else in this fucking
shithole, can we invent joy? Franky, in his alley, without
moving from his chair, he gave life, meaning, a language, an
aspiration to all of Grand Rue; to the alleys, to Doriane, to
Danilo whom I miss—damn I miss you, my friend—to a
beautiful, "burdened" woman, to a girl who made a mistake
by choosing the city over trees, to the mothers in the alley
who beat on their kids, misplacing their anger and missing
their true target, to the millions of miracle-seekers looking
to make a life for themselves because the one they have is
not what we call a life. And when you can't make the life you
want for yourself come true, you invent one in your dreams,
in blues, you invent a sea, a sky, love that doesn't resemble a
prison, plains filled with moscato mangoes, sapodillas to
your heart's content, birds protecting you with their wings,

paths that lead to a lakou where nobody has it out for anyone, with little girls climbing trees, and adults telling them
stories. And the little girls correct the adults' stories, which
sometimes lack audacity and imagination. And life, if you
have a little bit of intelligence, you tell yourself that if you
can invent it in your dreams, then maybe one day you could
make your dreams come true. Franky painted life in shades
of blue and gave branches to dying trees, he threw out fenc-
es, bars, and borders, liberated people from their prisons,
replaced the asphalt with the sea and the dust with a gentle
wind. Seer or not, Franky updated him, his Antoine of Gommiers. He painted him anew. And repainting a person is
worth more than repainting some old, two-story building
on Grand Rue. Repainting a person so that we'll finally realize that it's true, if you continue in the error of your ways...
So then what the fuck does it matter if it's a fable! And you,
Mr. President, in all these books in their beautiful rows, do
you discriminate between reality and fiction? Between facts
and dreams, there's room for the mysterious. Even when the
mysterious is a human invention." These were things I didn't
dare say. Nobody ever taught me how to talk to a President.
Maître Cantave wasn't a President, and all that I knew to say
to him was, "Yes, sir" and "He's doing well, sir. He'll certainly come by tomorrow, sir," when Franky had missed a day of
class due to his asthma.

The President wasn't in a hurry, his mind in his books,
maybe developing "a thesis." Pépé impatiently waited for his
response. And I worried that I'd made a mistake calling on
his services. I just wanted him to apply a little bit of pressure.
But Pépé and Triangle are incapable of doing anything a lit-

tle bit. The two had already stood up. I gestured for them to calm down. "No, not that." I hadn't told the President that we'd brought money with us. That Pépé, the king of dunces, who barely knew how to read, would be proud to contribute. To play the role of patron. A way of redeeming himself for having cut off Maître Cantave's arms. Since Triangle didn't know how to read at all, he was prepared to follow Pépé anywhere, in the slightest of his actions, including a mission to finance a fictional work of history. Nothing seemed to impress this little man in a bathrobe, nothing managed to take him out of his element. "It's a fable, or at least for the most part."

Yes, goddammit, it's a fable. But with all due respect, Mr. President, all of your great books, bound and arranged, all these little marvels in your room of wonder, who gives a shit about the veracity of the details if they don't lead you down a path? I didn't find the right words to explain things of a higher order. My thoughts were too simple, so I kept them to myself. We got up to leave. Pépé and Triangle were pissed. Gangsters have very short lives, so their time is precious. It's a sign of disrespect to call on them for help and then tell them to do nothing. "Thank you, Mr. President, sorry to bother you." He accompanied us on the way out. The TV was off. The bucket of ice and the bottle of whiskey had disappeared. The woman must be a dutiful wife and put them away. Maybe it was written in their marital contract, or the fruits of a tacit agreement. Your books, my living room, to each their own. The toy, protected by a door that must lead to a bedroom, started barking again, furiously. From inside, came the woman's voice: "Everything all right, mon

chéri? — "Yes, my love. I'm walking these gentlemen out."
— "Don't forget to put everything away if you've gotten
something out." The wealthy have the luxury of privacy in
their homes. It's not like in the alley, where without asking
for it, you know everything about everyone's life. We hadn't
come by for a little voyeurism. We walked closer to the door.
Outside, Speedy had already turned on the engine. And I
asked, just in case, just to see if Maître Cantave was right,
if the prize Franky won for composing his Mother's Day
poem, if he hadn't earned it, if my brother really knew how
to create with words, if Antoine's life story that occupied all
of his time wasn't at least a little bit worth it, if only for his
elements of style. The President replied that it was a little
outlandish (another one of these words that goes over my
head). A glimmer in his eyes, like the day of his conference
presentation, when he was elaborating "his thesis." He added
that he should start a collection called: "Myths and legends."

It felt strange to us, to all of us, modest chronicler, that we so often spoke of Antoine from Gommier's predictions, but nobody thought to ask him, or to ask ourselves, why he saw fit to share them. Normally, people hide their knowledge or revelations, only revealing them if they can gain some kind of advantage, a patent certificate or property rights, a street that bears their name or their own bust in a public square.

Should we not interpret Antoine of Gommier's predictions not as the description of an inevitable future, but as a reminder that the future is only what we make it. An altogether banal statement, a reflection within everyone's reach. But the human way is to forget what they know, a peasant from the plains of Gommiers, aided by divinities, raised in the school of the mysterious, or simply blessed with a beautiful intelligence, took it upon himself, not to teach us to surrender to the inevitable, but instead that when we allow the trees to die, it is vain to hope the return of their foliage, that every trap that closes on nature destroys it, that when we make a living

being into a weapon we mustn't be surprised when they kill...
These things remain true from continent to continent, from
archipelago to archipelago, from the plains of Gommiers to
the alleys of Grand Rue, whose true name is Boulevard Jean-
Jacques Dessalines.

Beyond the theatrics and linguistic flourishes so dear to
Antoine of Gommiers, we retain three things from him.

The interest he had in children, in whom he appeared to
find his true interlocutors.

The fact that no institutional power sought to valorize
him. Antoine of Gommiers did not inspire colloquia, nor
monuments. He is a legend laying in the dirt. Kept alive in
tap taps, in poor neighborhoods. Perhaps because the powerful
do not appreciate the mysterious. Perhaps because they know
that there is no other mystery in life other than what we choose
to do with it and ourselves, and they refuse to elect a figure
who reminds us of these facts.

The third thing, and it is that which interests us most as
chroniclers, is this—authentic or apocryphal documents,
dubious sources, or verifiable references—we never record the
passage of beings. Nothing else but the truth and untruths we
hope to extract. To each their mysteries and revelations in
this foreign war which is this act of language. This is why it
is both vain and useful to say: "If you continue in the error of
your ways..."

Which one of us had the idea of leaving the alley to go walk along Grand Rue? I don't know. When Franky and I were kids, so many things occurred to us at the same time that we never worried about the author or the source. Antoinette blamed me for the worst. Even if I suffered the consequences, Franky and I secretly laughed at this assignment of roles which was meant to split in half something that was, somewhere in our minds, instinctively one. It's nighttime, and we're the coauthors of this outing without importance or purpose. Maybe we miss each other after cooping ourselves up too long with one another in such a close space. Maybe we left in order to better come back to each other. There's little to see on Boulevard Jean-Jacques Dessalines. From time to time, a vehicle driving too fast, almost flying, with fear giving its wheels wings. Rare pedestrians. A drunkard wobbling forward, bracing himself against the walls, hurling insults at the ghosts living in his mind or at the drivers moving too fast to hear them. A few prostitutes.

The vehicles' headlights suddenly shine light on a face which shows the traces of a massacre. The evidence of old wounds that no one thinks to count. Death alone will come along to close them. Maybe they are a bunch of Antoinettes whose bodies were made of cheap wares. Without a great, great uncle entering into the legend. Neither a wise enough son to take their beatings and give them a little bit of power. Nor a son crazy enough to write them poetry and invent beauty for them. None of the women resembled Doriane. She left the alley and is perhaps making a childhood for herself somewhere else. Maybe she's going out with men her age. If you have a little luck, you can skip steps and decide one day to go back in time, to take the time to recognize what you missed by responding to the demands of the moment. Not far from the building from which Franky had fallen, a boy is sitting on the sidewalk. I don't know if Franky or I had the idea of helping him. I stopped pushing his chair. I tried to walk closer to the child. Slowly. So as not to scare him. But his fear had already settled, and he bolted and disappeared, engulfed by an alley. I went back to the chair. I don't know if Franky became lighter or if the chair rolled better than before, but my arms didn't strain. I could've walked like that for a long time. Maybe the chair has a soul of her own and knows that we'll soon replace her. With the President's check, we're going to buy a chair. Franky is precious, always looking for *le mot juste*. He prefers to say "wheelchair." Maybe we can't agree on everything. I'm the one who pushes. So maybe we can share the naming rights. He says "wheelchair" and I say "chair." Buying a chair or a wheelchair. Paying back Savior so that he can continue mixing work with pleasure. I need to find a lamp. Franky has so many projects. And the ceiling lamp poorly lights his table. Projects. And "a thesis." He says that there are so many legends that don't make it on Métro-Machin, so many stories left lying on the ground that blend disappointment and hope, good and evil, dreams and reality. That's where he needs to go looking so that words can bring about change. We walk in front of the bank. It doesn't look like much now, but very early tomorrow, it'll be inundated with miracle-seekers. I'll have to be there. To check them out and fill out their slips. It's time to turn around and go back home. I apply some pressure to the chair's handles, Franky some pressure to the wheelchair's wheels. It's the same movement and the same object. The same intention. Another thing we do together without having to work at it. Like in the souvenir from our childhood, the picture with our initials on the front of our hats. We continue down the alley. We go back inside. Each of us our own half. He wants to talk. I have a feeling he's going to want to take me onboard his frenzy of rhetorical devices. He starts. "Anacoluthon, catachresis." But I had a question and interrupted him.

"I know you've made up a lot of stuff. But there's one thing I want to know."

"Just one?"

"Yeah. This Grandma Hortense, did she really exist?"

"Why do you want to know?"

"Considering all the beatings she cost me..."

TRANSLATOR'S NOTE AND GLOSSARY

Lyonel Trouillot's novel, *Antoine of Gommiers,* is set between the cramped alleys of Port-au-Prince and the nostal-
gic, bluish hues of the Southern province of Grand Anse.
In the French edition, Trouillot frequently uses Haitian
Creole words. Sometimes these words are italicized and
glossed at the end of the novel, and others are transliterated into French and left out of the glossary. In this translation, I have avoided italicizing Haitian Creole words because they are as much a part of Haitian life as the realities
depicted in the novel. I have also rendered transliterated
Creole words in standard Haitian Creole orthography,
which has increased the number of Creole words in the
novel. Most of the time, the author provides a quick gloss
immediately following the use of a Haitian Creole word,
so I have imitated that process in my translation, hoping

that this will invite readers into the novel and the Haitian language. Similar to the French edition, we have provided a glossary, but we have elected not to signal anywhere in the text that a glossary appears. We hope people will read the text, and perhaps stumble upon the glossary later, or that curious readers might go in search of a glossary and find it waiting for them here. It is our way of saying, as Ti Tony puts it when he and Franky are being pushed out to sea, "seek, and you shall find."

Oungan – a male spiritual leader in the Vodou religion

Frenn – a small, makeshift knife

Estera – a show-off

Kolonn – a dear, close friend

Bòlèt – the local lottery in Port-au-Prince

Tap tap – a local and regional mode of transportation in Haiti, often a modified pick-up trucks or a small van

Bòlèt bank – a selling point for lottery tickets and numbers

Goud – the Haitian national currency, spelled *gourde* in French

Lakou – the ancestral, familial, or spiritual yard space in Haiti. A lakou can mean many things, sacred and profane, such as the courtyard of a single-family home, a group of interconnected homes, or a community of Vodou practitioners.

Tchala – a Haitian book of numbers and numerology

Malatyonn – either a lucky number or a number that is expected to win, but doesn't

Akra – a Haitian fritter, often made of malanga or taro

Blan – a foreigner, a white person, or a stranger

Mabi – a plant used to make a foamy alcoholic beverage

Kalalou djondjon – a Haitian stew featuring Chicken and okra.

Kavalye Pòlka (1984) – is a play by Syto Cavé about two men, Loreyal and Fatal, and their peregrinations throughout Port-au-Prince

"Lanmè Pòtoprens" – a poem by Georges Castera set to music by Wooly Saint Louis Jean.

Ounfò – a Vodou temple

Ounsi – a female apprentice to an oungan, a Vodou leader

Agouti – a tiny, shrew-like rodent

Mabouya – a lizard that lives around stone walls

AUTHOR BIOGRAPHY

Lyonel Trouillot is a novelist and poet in French and Haitian Creole, as well as a journalist and professor of French and Creole literature. His other novels in English translation include *The Children of Heroes* and *Street of Lost Footsteps* with the University of Nebraska Press as well as *Kannjawou* also by Schaffner Press. He lives in Port-au-Prince, Haiti.

TRANSLATOR BIOGRAPHY

Nathan H. Dize is Visiting Assistant Professor of French at Oberlin College. His translations include the following novels: *The Immortals* by Makenzy Orcel (SUNY Press), *I Am Alive* by Kettly Mars (UVA Press), *Antoine of Gommiers* by Lyonel Trouillot. Nathan's publications and translations have appeared in *archipelagos journal, Caribbean Quarterly, Francosphères,* the *Journal of Haitian Studies, The Southwest Review, Transition,* and *Words Without Borders*.